YOU'LL NEVER KNOW I'M HERE

KIERSTEN MODGLIN

KIERSTEN
MODGLIN

Cover Design by Kiersten Modglin
Copy Editing by Three Owls Editing
Proofreading by My Brother's Editor
Formatting by Kiersten Modglin
Copyright © 2023 by Kiersten Modglin.
All rights reserved.

First Print and Electronic Edition: 2023
kierstenmodglinauthor.com

To the book people.
The ones who fall in love with fictional characters, who cry over losses that only exist on the page, and who spend every night reading just "one more chapter" over and over again.
This one's for you.

"No man chooses evil because it is evil; he only mistakes it for happiness, the good he seeks."

-MARY WOLLSTONECRAFT

CHAPTER ONE

> If this were a thriller novel, we'd all be dead by the end of the weekend.

I glance down at the message from Mara as it comes in, smirking to myself before I dart across the street. She's not wrong, I guess. Our weekend plans would make the perfect plot for one of the thrillers we love so much.

I shove my phone into my purse, making a mental note to respond to it when I get out of the interview, and stare up at the bookstore in front of me.

Spines and Wines.

My fingers are like icicles as I squeeze them into fists, pulsing them twice before I pull the ends of my hair over my shoulders, smoothing it down and puffing out a breath.

It's going to be fine.

They're going to love you.

My sister's voice rings in my ears. Tucking my purse over my arm, I stride toward the door of the bookstore and pull it open. The place is cozy, with plants hanging in the windows and warm, wooden shelves as far as the eye can see.

A woman behind the counter, with a golden hoop piercing through her nose and her orange hair cut into a mullet, smiles at me. "Welcome in."

"Hi." I approach the counter, where a fat, gray tabby cat lies, purring happily as the woman strokes her side. "I'm here for an interview."

"Oh, right." Her eyes widen along with her smile. "I'm Mary, the manager. Nice to meet you."

My worries fade instantly, already at ease in her presence. "Nice to meet you, too. I'm Lena."

"Can I get you anything to drink?" She points at the oversized chalkboard behind her with their options painted in pretty, white script. Tea, coffee, wine, and beer.

"I'm okay. Thank you, though." My stomach rumbles, and I pray she doesn't hear it, too self-conscious to drink during the interview. "It's so cute in here."

She smiles, glancing around the room lovingly, and it's so completely obvious how much she adores the place. "I could die happy here," she says with a laugh. "*And* if I don't get a new employee soon, I just might." She rubs her hands together with a deep inhale, looking around at the counter. "Okay, cool. Well, if you want to browse the shelves or have a seat, I'll let him know you're here."

"Him?" *Shoot.* She's not the one interviewing me. Just like that, my anxiety is back. I relaxed too soon.

"Oh, right. Yes. Our owner." Her smile goes somewhat stiff. "He's... Well, you'll see. He likes to do the interviews himself. I'll tell him you're here, and he'll be right out." She picks up the phone to her right and presses a button.

asked you what to read." He leans forward over the table, challenging me.

"Well, what do you like?"

"Never read a book before," he says with a quick shake of his head. "No idea where to start. Come on." He snaps his fingers in quick succession. *Snap, snap, snap.* "Recommend something, Ms. *Full of Recommendations.* What's *in*?"

Sweat gathers at my hairline as I stare at him in utter disbelief that this is happening. "Um, well, if you prefer thrillers, Riley—"

"I don't know what I prefer. I just told you." He stands up from the table, shaking his head. "Thank you for your time, Ms. Ortega."

"Wait. What just happened? Are we done?" I follow him with my eyes as he walks away.

"I'm afraid so. I've learned all I need to. Feel free to ask for a coffee on your way out. On the house."

With that, he disappears in between the shelves of books. I stare at his path in complete shock. Then the anger hits.

What kind of interview was that?

What the hell is his problem?

I stand, gathering my purse and pulling on my jacket, and jump when I hear Mary's voice behind me.

"Sorry about him."

I turn, accepting the coffee cup she's handing me. "Is he always like that?"

"A ray of sunshine, you mean?" she asks with a chuckle. "Most of the time, yeah. I should've warned you, but I didn't want to give you...er, what's the opposite of rose-colored glasses?" She laughs again. "Doesn't matter." She waves away the question when I don't answer. "He's a good boss. Pays well, isn't too picky about days off. He just wants things done his way."

"Well, it doesn't seem like I'll have to worry about that," I say with a sigh, glancing at the door. "Thank you, though. And thank you for this." I lift up the cup of coffee.

"No problem." She steps back and turns away, then spins to face me again. "Oh. The answer is *Of Mice and Men*, by the way."

I stare at her.

"To the recommendation question," she clarifies. "I got it wrong, too. His dad is the one who started this place years ago, and it was his favorite book. He always told Memphis —who swears by it now—it's the universal book. The one anyone and everyone can read and enjoy." She shrugs. "Not sure how true it is. I haven't read it myself. But don't tell him that."

I smile at her. "Our secret."

And then I'm off, just as unemployed and pathetic as I was when I arrived.

CHAPTER TWO

When Thursday rolls around, I've all but forgotten about my terrible interview in favor of the excitement I feel about my weekend getaway.

The house where I'll be staying with my five closest internet friends is a grand old estate. We haven't met in person yet, but the six of us are what you might call *book influencers.* We have various accounts to promote the books we're reading and to celebrate books in general. We're some of the best, if I do say so myself. All blue-check verified, and authors and publishers often gift us books.

But that's not why we do it, of course. At least, it's not why I do it. I meant what I said in my interview. I love books. I love the way they smell, the weight of them in my hands. As a child, they took me away from what I considered a dull existence into some of the most amazing and beautiful worlds. Books have saved my life on more than one occasion, distracted me, given me something to hold onto in the darkest points of my life. And now they've brought me five new friends whom I'm just minutes from meeting.

We drive along the winding roads, passing one dilapidated house after the next. A few have boards up over their windows. One is missing a front door entirely. Several yards are overgrown, despite the cool November weather, signaling that they haven't been taken care of in months.

Maybe all summer.

Seeing me staring in the rearview mirror, the driver says, "The area you're staying in isn't as bad as this."

I worry about whatever face I was making that clearly told him what I was thinking.

"It's just an old town. Lots of people lost their houses, others can't keep up with repairs."

"You live here?" I ask. I assumed he lived closer to the town where he picked me up from the airport, nearly an hour away from here.

"I moved away," he says quickly. Proudly, even. "But then my mom got sick. I had to come back to help her out." He turns on his blinker, slowing down. "I work at the little market downtown now. And the gas station."

"Oh, wow."

He nods, pushing his glasses up on the bridge of his nose. "Yeah, well, as you can probably guess, I don't do much with ridesharing. You're probably my first request in six months." He chuckles. "But hey, if you need anything, the little downtown is within walking distance. There's not much, but you'll find the basics." Leaning forward, he turns down the country song playing on the radio.

"Okay, cool. Good to know."

"Milk, bread, some snacks, toilet paper. That sort of thing."

I draw in my lips, bobbing my head without a clue what to say next. "Awesome."

"Just know that everything around here closes down by five. Some even earlier in the winter. So get out during the day or you'll have to call for a ride to Paducah. I think I might be the only driver for this area, to be honest, and I work all weekend."

"Wow," I muse. "That's so wild to think about." I'd assumed everyone was flying in and booking a rideshare, but now I wonder if everyone else drove in or managed to rent a car. I'm just a month shy of being old enough to without paying an additional fee for my age.

As we pull onto the street, and the house comes into view, it's exactly how it looked in the pictures Ethan sent over. Ridiculously big. Presidential, even. The old bed and breakfast is colonial and well-maintained, surrounded by a knee-high, black, wrought iron fence.

"You have family here or something?" my driver asks, pulling me out of my thoughts.

"No," I tell him, though he's already asked me once. It's as if he doesn't believe me. "Just a few friends."

"It's a small town," he says with a whistle. "Real small."

I study the four white pillars on the grand front porch as the car pulls onto the paved driveway to the side of the house. The manicured lawn is full of young saplings and small hedges. From what I remember from the listing, when the owners of the bed and breakfast died, this house fell into disrepair. After the current owners bought it, they had to put a lot of money into fixing it up to be livable again. I suspect the fresh landscaping is another sign of the work and care the owners put into making this the vacation rental it is now—a small attempt at reviving what is clearly a dead town.

After all, this tiny town doesn't have much more than a grocery store, two gas stations, and a handful of restaurants from what he told me on the ride in and the limited research I did before arriving. I can't imagine it has much use for vacation rentals—who would be vacationing here?

If it wasn't for the fact that this was near the midway point for all of us, and Ethan had been able to find a house big enough for each of us to have our own room at an affordable price, I'd never have known it existed.

The driver pulls the car to a stop near the back of the house and turns around to look at me. "This is it."

"Thanks." I reach for the door handle and step out of the car, shocked by the temperature difference. Chills line my skin. It's so much colder here than I'd expected. *Isn't Kentucky supposed to be the South? I thought it didn't get cold here.*

The driver steps from the car and unloads my bags from the trunk, passing them off to me with a wave of his hand. "Have a good one."

"You, too," I say, pulling up the handle on my suitcase and rolling it across the lawn. I check the arrival email from the rental company for the door code as I approach the back porch and, with it entered, step into the house.

"Yo, someone's here!" a voice shouts down the hall before I have a chance to take in the tall ceiling with a linear crack leading to the antique chandelier or the wooden staircase and what appears to be hand-carved banister ahead of me. It's beautiful and timeless all at once, perfectly antique and yet still modern and kept up.

The sound of footsteps head in my direction, and I await them anxiously—sudden, unexpected nerves filling my stomach. I run a hand through my hair. I didn't think I'd be nervous meeting these people after spending hours and, ultimately, years calling them friends.

"There she is!" A man who I assume is Austin rounds the corner and holds out his arms for me. He has a mess of wild, curly brown hair and equally dark eyes, a stark contrast to his pale skin. Mostly, he's exactly what his profile suggests. "Lena?"

A smile spreads to my lips as he moves toward me. "Yes, hi! It's so nice to finally meet you."

He wraps me in a hug, and I catch a whiff of the cologne he's wearing—something peppery and warm.

"I'm Austin," he says, confirming my suspicion. "Paper-BoundAustin." He rattles off his username, in case I was unsure. "Guys, this is Lena. LitwithLenaO." He spins around so I get a clear picture of the two men walking up behind him. "Lena, this is Logan—BooksWithLoganC"— he gestures toward the shorter man with buzz-cut blond hair and expressive eyebrows—"and Memphis—Bookish-ReedReads."

My heart plummets as I lay eyes on the familiar dark hair and olive skin.

No.

No. No. No. No. No.

This has to be a joke.

"You..." The word escapes my throat without conscious thought. It's impossible.

The man in front of me appears equally shocked and confused to see me. His jaw clenches, and his Adam's apple bobs.

"What are you doing here?" I ask, staring at the man whom I last saw storming away from me in his bookstore... and haven't heard from since.

"You two know each other?" Austin asks, pointing between us with a brow quirked down. "I mean, besides from online."

"Sort of," I say, not quite sure how to explain our non-relationship.

"I don't know her from online," Memphis says at the same time.

"Oh, really? You guys'll have to follow each other," he says. "Her content is phenomenal. You follow Logan, right?" He points to Logan, who has yet to say a word. Memphis nods. "Do you follow everyone, Lena?"

"Mm-hmm," I say, hardly looking his way. "I think so. But I didn't know you were BookishReedReads. We've never talked." I look at Austin with a sheepish frown. "I didn't realize he was part of the group." *How did I not know?* I hate to sound like this is a clique, but the six of us have become pretty close over the last few years. The idea of someone new coming in is hard enough, but the fact that it's *him* is more than I can bear. Suddenly, I want nothing more than to go home.

"I'm not. I was a last-minute addition," Memphis says, though he's looking at Austin. "Actually, I was in the process of being invited when we met, though I'm using the word *invited* loosely, since it was more like *coerced*."

"Right. He's replacing Ethan," Austin explains with a drawn-out breath. "I forgot to say that."

My anger dissipates, completely forgotten. "Wait. *What?* Ethan isn't coming? Why? Since when?" I ask, whipping my head around to look at Austin. "We just spoke last week, and he was still coming then. No one told me the plans had changed." Ethan, the glue of our group and the person who convinced me to become a book influencer years ago, is the only reason I'm here. He's the one who suggested this get-together, who booked the place, and who brought us all together. How can he not be here? And why wouldn't he tell me?

"Sorry," Austin says with a regretful grimace on his face. "I assumed you knew. He had something come up at the last minute and couldn't make it. He told me he was going to send everyone a message, but I'm sure he didn't mean to miss you if he did. It was super last minute. A family emergency. Anyway, he suggested I invite someone else, and Memphis was at the top of the list. I didn't realize the two of you...um, had history."

"We don't," Memphis and I say at the same time.

From where he stands, Logan shuffles in place and shoves a hand into his pocket.

Austin runs a hand over the back of his neck. "Right. Okay, well...are we good, then? Or..."

"It's fine," I say quickly. "It'll be fine. Where's everyone else? Has Mara gotten here yet?" I just need to get out of this space and take a moment to process all of this.

"Nope, it's just us so far. Still have a pretty good pick of rooms, though." He points above his head. "They're all on the second floor. Need a hand with your bags?"

"I've got 'em, but thanks." I pull my bags closer to me, still upset by the sudden change in plans. I hope Mara and Paulette get here soon. It's silly, I guess, but I can't help feeling out of place in a house full of men. Especially a house full of men who are, for all intents and purposes, still strangers.

While we've all interacted online for a few years, or at least a few months in the case of Logan and me, this weekend, our getaway together in a peaceful vacation rental, was meant to be the first chance for us to really get to know each other. Now, I'm wishing I'd just said no in the first place.

I climb the two sets of stairs on my way up, denying, even to myself, that I'm trying to hear the men's voices down below. It doesn't matter, though. I can't hear a word. They're talking so softly, it must be about me.

I hate that I already feel so out of place. I've always been jealous of the people who fit in wherever they go, who can find friends in the grocery store checkout line and in the doctor's office waiting room. I've never been that person, no matter how hard I try. And now, just when I felt like I finally had somewhere I belong, Memphis's unexpected presence has me feeling out of sorts again. I hate that I'm letting him do that.

I shouldn't. I like Austin and Logan enough, and they seem to like me. They're always helpful and interactive on my social media, and we've done a few promos and collaborations together in the past. I feel like I know them, but in reality, I don't. And, obviously, they're chummy with Mr. *Of Mice and **Mean*** Bookstore Owner down there, which makes me feel even more like an outsider, as if he's come in

and overtaken the friend group I've worked so hard to culti-
vate and be a part of.

At the top of the stairs, there's a long hallway with
several doors. To my left, at the end of the hallway is a single
half-bath. The two doors closest to the bathroom have been
shut. Directly in front of me, there are three rooms with
their doors still cracked open and another that's been closed
at the end of the hallway to my right. Not willing to risk the
odds of sharing a wall with Memphis, I choose the bedroom
in the center of the three open doors.

Pushing the door open all the way, I'm hit by the
slightly stale scent that tells me this room has been closed
up for quite some time. There's a queen-sized bed in the
center of the room covered by an old quilt that appears to
be hand-stitched. Everything is very much on theme with
the old age of the house. The walls are painted white with
cherry-stained wood trim. There's no television, and in the
corner of the room there's a decorative, antique wash basin
and pitcher. On the opposite side of the bed, there's a door
and, when I open it, I find a small bathroom with tile floors,
a pedestal sink, and a stand-in shower.

It's nothing spectacular, but it's clean, and the house is
beautiful. Plus, it's a weekend of privacy, something that
seems to be a thing of the past since moving back into my
parents' house.

I don't know how single people afford life anymore.
How is anyone supposed to meet the requirement of
making three times the rent when the rent is astronomical?
And the idea of getting a roommate at twenty-four years
old feels ridiculous. I'm supposed to be an adult now. Independent. I don't want to have to go back to labeling my

food and waking up to strangers in my apartment from unexpected sleepovers. I'm supposed to take care of myself, have my own life, though I'm not sure living with my parents is much better.

I lift my bags and place them on the bed. The antique, metal frame groans with their weight, which gives me little confidence in its ability to hold me.

I open my suitcase and pull out a bag of chewy Nerds, stuffing a few into my mouth. Instead of unpacking the rest of my things, I unlock my phone and pull up my text message thread with Ethan, ready to check on him. As much as I hate that he's not here, I'm also worried about what sort of family emergency would've caused him to miss this weekend after he worked so hard to plan it.

> Hey! Just found out you aren't coming this weekend. I'm so sad to miss you! Hope everything's okay.

I read the message twice, trying to decide if it sounds too needy or like I had too much riding on finally meeting him. I have no idea if he had the same hopes for this weekend as I did. After all, we've only ever spoken across social media and via text. Am I crazy for thinking there might be something between us?

The answer is yes, most likely.

I hit send without allowing myself to second-guess it too much and then tuck my phone back into my jeans pocket before I begin to unpack.

I've nearly gotten all of my clothes unpacked and placed into the drawers of the small dresser in front of the bed when I hear a woman's voice downstairs. My heart soars with relief, and I dart out of the room, pulling the door closed behind me.

I slow my steps as I reach the stairs, careful not to trip as I round the corner. The moment I see her, my worries disappear.

"Mara!" I call, waving a hand at her. "Oh my god!"

She pushes the expensive-looking sunglasses up onto her head, blowing a piece of hair out of her face as she takes in the sight of the room before her eyes land on me. She grins with her hands on her hips.

"Well, hey there, stranger!" she says with a laugh. Though I've heard her voice in the live videos we've done together and in the voice memos we've exchanged, hearing it in person is something totally different. Warmer.

I pull her into a hug with sudden tears brimming my eyes. How is it that my best friend in the world is someone I'm just meeting for the first time?

She hugs me back just as tightly, and I hear her voice crack as she says, "I can't believe you're here."

"I can't believe *you're* here," I say, pulling away to get a good look at her.

"Awww! Well, I can't believe you're both here," comes Austin's voice from down the hall, albeit high-pitched and played up, like he's a Southern Belle. "Oh my gosh!"

He enters the room, fanning his face dramatically, and Mara laughs, launching toward him. Her black hair bunches up around the neck of her sweater as she hugs him, and I can't help feeling jealous.

"Memphis Reed, in the flesh!" she cries when she sees the asshole round the corner. "And here I thought vampires only came out at night."

Am I the only one who doesn't know him this well?

"Hey, Mara." He gives her a small smile and a one-armed hug that doesn't at all match her energy. "Good to see you, too."

She takes her sunglasses off of her head. "I thought you weren't going to make it."

"He strong-armed me," Memphis says, jutting an elbow toward Austin.

"You knew Ethan wasn't coming?" I ask her.

She looks over at me. "Yeah. You mean you didn't?"

"No, I had no idea."

She pulls out her phone, and I watch as she opens her social media app. "He sent me a message...what, like, Monday, I guess. Yeah, Monday." She spins the phone around so I can see the message. "He said his grandmother died."

"Oh." My stomach drops. "Oh, god. That's terrible."

"Yeah, I didn't want to tell his business or whatever," Austin says, his head tilted downward.

"Shoot." Mara covers her mouth. "I wasn't thinking."

"He won't care that I know," I say. I want to believe it's true, but why am I the only one he didn't tell? Then again, how dare I expect him to tell me anything when he is going through such a tragedy?

"Of course not," she agrees. "He only messaged me to ask if I knew anyone who'd want to take his place on the trip. You know, so we wouldn't all have to pay more or have him pay for a trip he couldn't come on. But I didn't. No one I asked could make it on such short notice."

"Which is probably when he reached out to me,"

Austin says. "That was Monday night, because I reached out to Memphis on Tuesday."

The day of my interview.

"Logan never heard from him either, but I convinced Memphis to come by Tuesday morning, so that was probably why he didn't reach out to you guys. I'm sure he just had a lot on his plate."

He's probably right. It should make me feel better that at least I wasn't the only one, but somehow it doesn't. The fact that I was so far down his list only further proves we were never as close as I thought we were. It's all been in my head.

"Yeah, of course," I say eventually. "No big deal. I'm just glad it all worked out."

"Okay, so what are we doing? Where are the rooms? Why isn't there wine yet? Is everyone here?" Mara asks, practically all in one breath. "I can't believe this is happening! Ah! You guys are real!"

"Rooms are upstairs," Austin and I say at the same time. He smiles and gestures toward me, letting me finish the sentence. "I'll show you the way."

I lead Mara upstairs, and along the way she talks my head off about the drive in and the fiasco she dealt with in airport security.

"I totally didn't know you don't have to take everything out of your bags now, so I was just taking it all out, and the man was like 'No! No! You don't do that anymore!' Like, hello? How was I supposed to know?"

I chuckle. "Yeah, seriously. I'm just glad they let you get on the plane."

"Please." She rolls her eyes, looping an arm through

mine. "I would've held onto a wing if they didn't. I was getting here one way or another."

In the hall, I show her the room choices she has left. "Here or there."

"Where are you staying?"

I point to my room in the middle. "This one."

"Okay, good. So we're together either way, then." She chooses the room to my left, and I follow her inside as she unpacks. When she places her bags down, I notice her bed frame doesn't squeak.

"This weekend is going to be so fun," she says with a sigh, dumping her duffel bag out in its entirety on the old quilt. She begins sorting through her makeup and clothing, none of which has been organized or folded. I chuckle to myself. She's exactly what I expected, and it's refreshing.

"If we don't all die," I tease, reminding her of the message she sent just a few days ago.

"Right." She winks. "So sad about Ethan, right?"

"Yeah." I sit down on the side of her bed. "Speaking of, how well do you know Memphis?"

Her head jerks up, her face serious. "Oh no. What'd he do?"

"Nothing."

Her brows shoot up.

"No, I mean, really nothing. We just...sort of met earlier this week."

"You mean you *met*, met?" She rocks her hips forward suggestively with a wink.

"No." I cover my mouth with a loud laugh. "God, no. Nothing like that. He interviewed me for his bookstore."

Her eyes widen. "He owns a bookstore? Do you get

discounts? Discounts you could share with your very best friend?" Before I know it, she's up on the bed, crawling toward me, her bottom lip stuck out in a pout. "Your best friend who loves you so much?"

"Well, I wouldn't know," I say, waving her off playfully. "Because he didn't hire me."

"That asshole." Her response is instantaneous. "We should kick him out. We should put shaving cream in his hand while he sleeps and tickle his nose with a feather. No! We should put his hand in warm water and make him pee the bed. Does that work? My cousin and I tried it on her younger brother when we were little, but I don't remember if it ever worked." She looks at me with wide eyes and shakes her head. "Sorry, what were we talking about? Memphis! Right. Ugh, asshole."

I toss my head back onto the pillow. "Yeah, well, it's fine. I just didn't realize he'd be here, and that makes this all a little bit awkward."

"I'm sorry." She winces. "What can I do? Want me to be the buffer all weekend? We can pretend he doesn't exist. I'm seriously the best at that. Memphis who?" She snaps her fingers and leans back on one leg dramatically.

"Shhh! Don't let him hear you. It's seriously not a big deal. I just didn't realize the two of you knew each other."

"Eh"—she waves her hand—"barely. We connected last year on that big Thanksgiving giveaway that ZoeBooks organized. Do you remember me telling you about that?"

"Yeah."

"So, he was one of the others involved in that. We've chatted a bit here and there, and then he messaged me yesterday sort of out of the blue to ask if I was coming to this and if I knew who else was."

"So, you told him I'd be here?" I ask, tension in my chest.

"Um, yeah, I guess so. Oh, what do you think that means? Maybe he wanted to see you again to apologize? Maybe he wants to *meet*"—her pelvis rocks forward playfully with the word—"you again."

"I doubt it. He probably just didn't realize who I am. I rarely post photos of my face online. Although, it's pretty funny that he's an influencer considering that when I told him this is what I do during my interview, he acted like it was ridiculous." I put on my best impression of him. "'I'm not interested in what's in, I'm interested in what's good.'"

She snorts, covering her nose and mouth. "Oh my gosh, it checks out. I can totally picture him saying that. He has the *I'm better than you because I read smart people books* vibe, for sure. Hey, speaking of that, what books did you bring?" She climbs back off the bed and begins to take things out of her second bag, which seems to be filled mostly with hardback books. "I brought practically everything on my fall TBR, plus a few favorites from the year that I haven't posted about yet. And I figure we can all mix and match books, too, so we can make extra content."

"Good idea," I say. "We have a few of the same." I point to her copy of Blakely Baldwin's newest book and the Cait Du Bois novel I just started. "But I have plenty in my room, too. We can go through them later."

"Awesome." She looks up, wiggling a brow at me. "So... since we *definitely* don't like Memphis, is it okay to say that Austin's pretty hot?"

"What?" I scoff, wrinkling my nose. "You think so?"

"Uh, yeah. He's got that...what's that guy from *American Horror Story*?" She taps a finger to her temple. "I can't think of his name. The actor who played...well, like, everyone." With a laugh, she goes on. "Uh, it's on the tip of my tongue. Peter? Peters? Evan Peters! Yes! He has that Evan Peters vibe. You know?"

I shrug one shoulder. "I guess I wasn't really paying attention, but sure."

"Were you not paying attention because you were too busy enemies-to-lover-ing with Memphis?"

I stick my tongue out. "I am not here to *pay attention* to anyone."

She shoves her fists into her sides. "Except me."

"Definitely you."

She chuckles, wadding up a few of her shirts and tossing them in a drawer. "I'm just saying. You're single now. Doesn't hurt to look."

"Yeah, well, last time I looked, I got my heart broken."

"Cheating asshole," she mutters under her breath.

"Besides, even if I was interested in Austin—*which I'm not*—he lives in Florida. It's not like anything could happen between us. I'd never see him, and long-distance relationships don't work."

"Easy there, Reverend. I'm not suggesting you marry the guy. I'm just saying...a weekend in a big house like this, you could have a little fun. And, if you don't plan to, maybe I will." She wiggles her shoulders, her tongue pressed to her teeth.

"Have at it," I tell her.

"You sure?"

"Positive. If you like him, go for it."

She grins. "Maybe I will."

I smirk and shake my head, looking away as we hear a new voice downstairs that can only belong to Paulette. The last arrival.

"Paulette's here. Guess that's all of us." Mara looks at me expectantly.

I grin and head for the door. "Guess so. Let the games begin."

She clears her throat and gives me a prim and proper look. "I believe you mean: Chapter One."

CHAPTER THREE

Once Paulette has unloaded her bags into her room, the group gathers in the dining room downstairs. It's a large, open room with wallpaper covering the top half of the walls, a fireplace on the far side of the room, and a chandelier dangling from the yellowing ceiling.

The hardwood floor is covered with an oversized rug with a pattern that reminds me of evil faces more than the flowers it's meant to be. Their features are distorted—a deep maroon color—and seem to be frowning at me.

From where I stand behind one of the dining room chairs around the table, I take in the sight of everyone.

Paulette is lying across one of the wingback chairs in the corner, her long legs draped over the arm. She's wearing a shirt with a portrait of two opossums on a magic carpet, with the words **I can show you some trash** around them. I know from her profile that she creates her shirts herself, which makes this even funnier.

"So, what should we do first?" Mara asks, bouncing up on her tiptoes, practically giddy with excitement.

"I don't know about y'all, but I'm starving," Austin says, looking around. "How are we going to do meals while we're here?"

"Good question," Mara says. "Everyone ordering their own? Or are we taking turns cooking and paying for everything? Are there any allergies here? Or sensitivities? I don't do well with dairy, but I can manage to avoid that in most things. Maybe we should go to the grocery store together and split the cost? I don't care either way, I just need to eat something."

"Same," Logan agrees, picking a piece of lint off the shoulder of his shirt. "Did anyone drive, by the way?" He looks around as everyone shakes their heads.

"Uber it is, then," says Paulette with a deep, goofy laugh. "Anyone want a special gummy before we go?" She lifts up a clear bag of gummy bears, and I don't have to ask what she means by *special*.

"I'm good." Memphis is the first to speak up.

Austin zips across the room, digging his hand in the bag and popping two in his mouth. "*Oh my god*, you're my hero. How did you manage to get those on the plane?"

She winks. "Never travel without 'em."

He closes his eyes as he swallows the treat, petting Paulette on the head. "I knew I liked you. We're going to get along just fine."

She pretends to bite at his fingers, and he pulls them away.

"Okay, well," Mara says, drawing our attention back to her with a clipped tone that only I seem to notice, "I passed a little grocery store, market-type place on my way in. We could easily walk to it and get a few things for the night if you want."

"Oh, right. My driver mentioned that," I pipe up. "I wanted to get some pictures down by the river anyway. Anyone else up for a walk?"

"I'll go." Paulette lifts her hand in the air, standing from the chair. She tugs at her shirt, tucking the bag of gummies back into her oversized purse, which is shaped like a chicken, and slipping it over her shoulder.

"Why don't we all go?" Austin asks, looking over at Memphis, who grumbles but doesn't answer.

"I'm in," Logan agrees.

"It's settled, then," I say. "Anyone who wants to go, let's go before it starts getting dark." I check the clock. It's just after three, which means the sun will begin setting within a few hours. "We'll get what we can, and if it's not enough, then tomorrow, we can call an Uber or cab to get us to the grocery store."

"Or we could have groceries delivered, maybe," Paulette says, tucking a piece of her light brown hair behind her ears, which I notice are sporting Cheez-It-shaped earrings, complete with realistic-looking granules of salt.

"Okay, cool." Austin sighs and shoves his hands into his pockets. "Let me grab some books from my room to take pictures of down by the water. Good idea, Lena."

Everyone heads upstairs at once to do the same, and when we return and meet downstairs, we're all carrying canvas bags with varying amounts of books inside them.

With our jackets on, we head out the door, and Austin presses the button to lock it behind us while Mara points in the direction she remembers seeing the store.

"It was just up over that hill in the distance. There's a small, little downtown area."

"Oh! Maybe they have a bookstore," Paulette cries, though she's already struggling with the weight of the bag in her arms.

"I don't think so," Mara says. "At least not on the main strip. I only saw the market and maybe a restaurant in what looked like an old tire shop. The rest of the buildings were boarded up."

"Remind me. Why did we pick this bustling oasis again?" Memphis asks, shocking me with the first full sentence I've heard from him in a while.

"Ethan picked it," Logan says. Beside me, Mara is humming a tune softly, though she seems almost unaware she's doing it.

"It was in the center of all of us," Austin adds. "Florida for me, Illinois for Lena—oh, and you, I guess—Colorado for Logan, Virginia for Mara, Michigan for him, and..." He pauses, looking at Paulette. "I wanna say South Car—"

"Georgia," she corrects. "I'm from Georgia."

"Right." He snaps his fingers and jumps up. "Uh, so close! Anyway, so, this little town in the middle of nowhere in Kentucky was sort of our meeting point..." His sentence trails off, getting lower and slower as he becomes distracted by something off in the distance. "Hey, do you guys dare me to climb that tree?" Before we can answer, he's off in a flash into the field and dangling from the lowest branch of the giant shade tree.

"Oh my god," Mara cries, covering her mouth. "Get down before you get hurt. I doubt they have any hospitals here for miles."

He swings back and forth faster. "Oh, come on, you big babies. Haven't you ever climbed a tree before?" He sticks out his tongue. We cross the field on our way to him, and he seems to be having so much fun it's nearly impossible to be frustrated.

"You're staining your pants," Logan points out, nodding toward the brown stains on the inner thighs of Austin's blue jeans.

"Come on, Paulette. What do you say? Show these old farts how it's done." His brows dance, egging her on.

She releases a loud, dramatic laugh, but it slowly dies off as if she'd been considering it. "I don't want to get hurt. I'm telling you I'm the most accident-prone person ever."

"I'll protect you, I swear." As he says the words, he loses his grip on the branch and drops to the ground in a second with a loud thud.

"Oh!" Mara calls out. "Are you okay?"

I bend down to help him to his feet, but he waves me away, sitting up and gazing at the sky as he dusts off his pants. "You gotta learn to live a little, you guys. I'm fine, see?"

"We should really get going," I remind him. "Before it starts getting dark."

"Okay, fine." His voice is breathy as he stands up, dusting off the seat of his pants. He pretends to be a grumpy old man as he walks through the field. "Here we go. Gotta get back before the streetlights come on."

"Uh, now I'm realizing this place doesn't even have streetlights," Paulette whines.

"Gotta love staying in the middle of nowhere," Logan

31

groans, swatting away an insect as it flies near him. He wraps his coat farther around himself with a shiver.

"Yeah, not really. I mean, we all flew in, right? So why would a halfway point even matter? If anything, this feels more out of the way," Memphis points out. "I'm just saying, my rideshare driver acted like I was the first person he'd ever had request a ride. *He* was asking *me* how things worked."

"Yeah, same," I agree.

Memphis looks as shocked by the admission as I am. Shocked that I'm agreeing with him for any reason. I instantly turn away and direct my attention to Mara.

"It's definitely not ideal. But I think Ethan said he got a good deal on this house. Plus, it's historic and pretty, and there's supposed to be really nice areas to take photos in."

"Exactly," she says, wrapping an arm around my shoulder. Since she's a bit shorter than I am—which is really saying something, as I'm usually the shortest person in the room—it's not an easy thing to do, and she eventually lets it drop. "It's perfect."

The walk to the small downtown is much like my drive to the house, filled with mostly old, run-down houses that look ready to collapse at any moment. After another few minutes of walking, we reach the market Mara told us about and make our way inside the small store. It's rustic in a way that's clearly not done in order to be on trend. The floors are wooden and creaky, and the shelves all have handwritten price tags. The options they have are somewhat limited, but they'll do for the night.

Each of us takes a basket, and we set to work grabbing snacks and easy items for breakfast. We've decided to split the cost of everything as equally as possible and switch up who's going to be cooking which meal for the remainder of the trip. Mara and Logan have agreed to take the first dinner shift, and the meal they're making is chili. Of course, with Mara, it can't just be regular chili. It will be what she's calling chili-cuterie. An entire board of options to go with the chili. I toss a jar of jalapeños into my basket, thinking about how much I cannot wait.

"Well, hello there." A voice startles me from behind, and I turn around to find an older man and woman staring at me. He's a few inches shorter than her and has a large bald patch atop his head. What little hair remains on his scalp is graying. His piercing blue eyes match hers almost entirely, though her hair has clearly been colored black and is held in place with what must be a massive amount of hairspray.

I smile at them awkwardly, thinking they must've mistaken me for someone else. "Um. Hi."

"I don't think we've seen you here before." The woman is latched onto her husband, one arm around his shoulders, the other placed on his chest. Her blue eyes widen as she glances in my basket and then at my bag. I'm trying not to be weirded out, but they are both giving me the creeps.

"Oh. Well, you wouldn't have. I'm... I'm just visiting."

"That's nice. Family in town, then?" the man asks.

"What's your name, dear?" his wife interrupts him.

"It's, um..." I swallow nervously. I'm probably being ridiculous, but something in me is saying I shouldn't give them my name. I glance beside them, but there is no way to get out of this aisle. They're blocking the exit, and behind me, there is only a wall. I scan the other aisles, seeing the familiar heads of my group members, but no one seems to have noticed our strange and uncomfortable interaction.

"She's with me."

I hear his loud voice from behind them seconds before he appears, his face unreadable, lips pressed into a thin line. Memphis squeezes past them and puts an arm around my shoulders, looking down at my basket. I resist the urge to shove him off of me out of pure shock.

"You found the crackers? Good, I've got everything else. You ready to go?"

I should say something now. Anything. Or shrug him off and demand he leave me alone, but I'm utterly speechless. Shocked by his actions and by his touch, which is all too comfortable, and I hate how aware of that I am.

"Um..." I manage to squeak out.

He looks up at the couple, searing them with his dark, impenetrable stare. "If you'll excuse us."

"Oh. Of course. Yes. It was nice to meet you both," the man calls after us as Memphis ushers me past them.

"Enjoy your visit," says the woman.

Memphis leads me down the aisle and toward the register before he takes his arm off of my shoulders without addressing what just happened or why he helped me. When we reach the counter, I unload my basket without a word.

"'Sup, guys?" Austin asks, appearing behind us without warning. His basket is loaded down with junk food, and he's already eating from a bag of chips. "Find everything?" he asks with his mouth full.

"Yup," Memphis answers for us both, setting his basket on the counter next to mine.

"Hey." Mara touches my back, and I realize the whole

group has now arrived at the counter. From across the room, I can still feel the strange couple's eyes on me, though I don't check to see if I'm right.

A middle-aged man appears behind the counter from a room in the back, smacking pink bubble gum between his teeth. "Oh, hello. Sorry about that." He hurries his pace on his way to us. "Find everything okay?"

"Yes, thank you," Mara says.

"You kids aren't from around here, are you? Don't think I've seen you before." He peers at us from behind thick lenses as he scans my items.

"No, just visiting," Mara answers.

He smacks his gum obnoxiously, strings of saliva trailing between his lips, and I fight against the urge to reach across the counter and close his mouth for him.

"What brings you to town? We don't get many visitors around here."

Somehow, the words feel like a warning, and I suddenly regret the jokes Mara and I have been making about how this whole getaway feels like a thriller plot.

"We're staying at the big house down the street. The old bed and breakfast." Logan points in the direction of the house.

I cringe and notice I'm not the only one. Austin and Memphis are both giving him deadly stares when I turn around to look his way. He looks sheepish and steps back.

"Oh, the old Buchanan place? I know the one. That one used to have a lot of life in it. Good to see it have guests again. How long are you kids in town?"

"Not long at all," I tell him.

"Just for a few days," Paulette says casually, perusing the

candy near the checkout. She adds two handfuls of candy bars to her basket. "It's a cute town."

"Been here all my life," he drawls with a chuckle under his breath. "*Cute* ain't a word I've ever heard to describe it."

Behind me, someone in the group stifles a laugh that quickly dies out. I force a smile and pass him my card, unsure of what to say. Rather than swipe the card, he holds it up to the light as if he might be checking to see if it's counterfeit, then whistles. "Lena Ortega... Lena, hm? That short for anything?" His brow lifts.

"Um, no. Just Lena."

He continues to eye me, then Memphis and Mara. "Where'd you say you were from again?"

"We didn't," Memphis answers before I can. "We're in a hurry. Can you just get us checked out so we can be on our way?"

The man looks at Memphis with an expression that scorches but swipes my card without another word.

Ten minutes later, we're walking out of the market with our groceries in plastic bags and on our way toward the river. Memphis has made no effort to bring up what happened back there, but I feel as if I need to address it.

I hurry my pace to catch up with him near the front of the group. When I move next to him, he barely glances at me from the corner of his eye, and I can't help noticing the small smirk on his lips.

"You didn't have to do that, you know?"

He looks straight ahead, squinting at the horizon. "Do what?"

"Help me get away from that couple."

He shrugs one shoulder and doesn't say anything for a

while. Then, surprising me, he says, "You looked uncomfortable."

"Yeah, probably overreacting. They were just... I don't know. I had a weird feeling about them. I'm sure they were just being nice."

"Who was being nice?" Austin asks, inserting himself into the conversation, somehow walking and spinning in circles at once.

"This couple that was trying to talk to me in the store back there. They sort of cornered me while I was in an aisle alone and were being really weird. I was worried they weren't going to let me walk away"—I look up at Memphis, who's staring straight ahead with determined fascination—"until Memphis came over and got me out of there."

"Weird how?" Mara asks, walking up next to me so we're all in a line now. "What were they doing?"

"I don't know. Mostly just asking me questions. But also staring at me in this strange way."

"What were they asking?" Austin trips on the gravel road and stops spinning, catching his breath.

"Just... I don't know. They were asking me where I am from, same as the cashier, but there was just something about them. They gave me the creeps." I shiver. "I can't explain it."

"Babe, trust your gut. Simple as that. If it said they were weirdos, it's 'cause they were. You should've told me, though. Caught my eye, gave me a little head nod. I would've fought someone." She flexes her arm, patting her bicep with a grin.

"It's all good now." I lean my head over onto her

shoulder briefly, then gasp as the river comes into view. "Oh, wow! Look!"

"Nice," Logan says, picking up his pace. "I call dibs on the tree as my first photo spot." A large oak tree sits near the shoreline, its branches bare and spindly against the darkening, gray sky, making it a perfect addition to any photo with a thriller novel. I suspect we're all thinking the same thing.

We make our way down to the water and split up, each pulling out our various books and posing them in different ways, snapping moody pictures against the desolate backdrop.

The sun seems to set quicker as I snap my last few photos—one against a pile of rocks and one held out in front of the water. Chills line my skin, even under my coat.

"It's starting to get dark, guys," Paulette says, trying to stand from the ground where she was taking a photo. Instead, she trips and lands face first. She lets out an uproarious laugh and slaps the ground. When she turns over, her shirt and jeans are smeared with mud, but she doesn't seem to mind. "And that's one way of making an exit."

"You okay?" Mara asks as she and I rush toward Paulette and help her up.

"I'm good." She dusts off the knees of her jeans. "Just clumsy."

"She's right," Austin says, appearing next to us. For a second, I think he's agreeing with her about being clumsy. "It's going to be dark soon. And, anyway, we should get back before the groceries spoil."

With everyone in agreement, we make our way toward the house. Just as we top the hill, something in the woods to our left—back behind the market and the small downtown area—catches my eye.

I freeze.

"What's wrong?" Mara asks. At the sound of her voice, everyone stops and turns back to face us.

I peer into the treeline, trying to spot whatever movement I just saw. "This is going to sound paranoid, but I think someone's out there."

"Out where? In the woods?" Austin asks, moving in front of us. Logan follows him.

"It looked like it. I thought I saw something out there a little while back, but...now I'm nearly positive I just did again. Like someone's following us."

Mara gives me a playful look. "Oh, wait. Haha. Very funny. You almost had me."

"Seriously? You're joking?" Memphis asks, his voice low and grumpy.

"No, I'm not. I swear. I saw something—someone—in the woods." I take a step forward as if trying to go for a closer look.

Austin puts a hand up behind us, herding us forward. "We should keep moving. We're almost to the house."

He stays in the back of the group, trying to pretend he's not afraid but when I look over my shoulder at him, I see him watching the woods with a gaze that tells me something else.

It's possible I'm not the only one who saw something, and either way, I'm not the only one afraid.

CHAPTER FOUR

When we get home, Mara and Logan set to work preparing our first meal while the rest of us hang out in the living room. I zip to my room to get my laptop and return to the empty spot on the couch to begin editing the photos I took down by the water, searching for a preset filter that will do the eerie background justice.

Nearly everyone else seems to be doing the same thing —Austin on his phone and Paulette on her laptop as well. It's just Memphis that can't seem to be bothered with the content he created. In fact, now that I think of it, I only saw him snap one or two pictures while we were down by the river. I'm sure he spent the entire time thinking about how shallow we all are. Instead of working, he has a paperback book open in his lap, one leg crossed over the other as he reads with a serious expression, clearly unbothered by the things I spend my days thinking about.

In a way, it must be freeing not to care so much. I can't remember the last time I read a book without thinking about how it would fit into my page's aesthetic or what sort of backdrop would look best with it. I'm not sure how to feel about that.

I wasn't always this way. That much I do know. There was a time when I started posting about books because I loved them. This was before the challenges asking me to share the books I hated, which phrases I'm tired of seeing in novels, and even bad reviews for books I've loved. A time when I only wanted to post about books because I loved them so much I wanted others to hear about them. Before it all became a popularity contest.

I remember when it all changed for me if I really think about it. When my page was really starting to grow, there was another influencer who posted similar content. A lot of our followers overlapped, and people started comparing us, both in good and bad ways. Comparing the posts we made about the same books. Comparing the challenges we participated in. Saying whose content they liked more—and it was usually hers.

I never wanted to compete with anyone.

Growing up with a sister who was practically perfect at everything from academics to sports, who then went on to have the perfect wedding and a beautiful family, all I've ever experienced is people comparing me to her, even when they don't mean to.

So, the experience of being compared to anyone else is triggering for me now. And that experience in particular has been really hard for me to overlook and move on from. Especially when the comments and messages comparing us or praising her continue to come in. Especially when I don't ever seem to get praise for anything alone. It's always check out Lena *and* Tae. *They're both so great.*

If you like Lena, be sure to check out Tae.

Lena, did you see Tae's review on this book? You guys have such similar thoughts! Really loved both of your takes.

Maybe I'm complaining over something silly, but it doesn't feel silly to me.

Sometimes it just really sucks to be constantly compared to someone you never asked to compete with. When you just want to be your own person and do your own thing, and everyone seems hell-bent against letting that happen.

Watching Memphis read his book without a care in the world reminds me of a simpler time when none of it mattered, and I could just read books because I loved them. Without thinking, I open the browser on my laptop and pull up the profile Austin told me is Memphis's.

BookishReedReads

The account only has around ten thousand followers—much fewer than the rest of us—but the content is actually impressive. Curated photographs all in front of the same background—nicely lit bookshelves, which I suspect must be in his store.

The books aren't ones I see talked about much. Some are older, some much newer. Independent authors. A lot of classics. Debut authors no one else is sharing. His taste is diverse and impressive.

Still, it's hard to picture him taking these photos or writing the corresponding book reviews that accompany them. It's hard to imagine him caring about anything enough to do so.

As if he can read my guilty thoughts, I look up to find him staring at me from behind the book he's reading—

something I've never heard of that looks literary and sophisticated.

It would probably go right over my head.

From the kitchen, I can hear Mara humming again over the sounds of them cooking—running water, meat sizzling in a skillet, a *chop, chop, chop* as someone cuts the vegetables. The scent of the chili is intoxicating, and my stomach growls at the thought of it.

"Oh man, people are already freaking out over this one." Paulette chuckles from behind her laptop. "That tree was such a good idea." She turns her screen around so we can see the way she made the branches on the cover of her latest read blend in nearly perfectly with the branches on the tree. It's a perfect shot from the ground, with the camera pointed up to really take in the branches as a whole.

"Love that shot," Austin says.

"Super cool," I agree.

My eyes dart to her then back to Memphis, who has returned his attention to his book. I close out of his account and focus again on editing the photo I'm working on.

Another half an hour goes by before Mara announces dinner is almost ready. Paulette and I close our laptops and return them to our rooms before meeting everyone else in the dining room. Passing through the kitchen, I spy Logan cleaning up what's left of their mess from preparing the meal—wiping down the counters and stove top and dusting crumbs into his palm.

"Smells delicious," I tell him to fill the awkward silence.

He smiles at me with a nod but offers nothing to the conversation.

In the dining room, Mara stands in a chair to snap a

photo of the spread she's laid out—shredded cheese, sour cream, oyster and saltine crackers, green onions, tortilla chips, jalapeños, and a few slices of avocado and lime.

"This looks amazing, Mara," I tell her, to which she does a little curtsy and jumps down from the chair.

"Thank you, daaah-ling," she drawls with a deep Southern accent, then bows. When she's done, we each fill our bowls from the pot in the center of the table. "And I made margaritas, too, so hope you all like them."

"Oh, margaritas and chili? Marry me and make me the happiest woman alive, Mara," Paulette says, dropping to her knee and bumping the chair beside her so it slams into the table. She laughs with her eyes closed, and Mara presses a kiss to her cheek.

"Why buy the cow when you can get the milk for free?" She winks, and Paulette slaps her butt playfully.

Memphis plops a mug of coffee down in front of his seat as everyone else pours a margarita from the pitcher.

Paulette watches as Mara drops two jalapeños in her drink, then does the same. "Oh, fancy. I think I'll try that." She takes a sip, blinking rapidly and patting her chest. She puffs out a breath. "Wow."

"You like it?" Mara asks with a grin.

Paulette nods, puffing out another breath. "It's delicious, duh. Just spicier than I expected." As she's sitting down, she asks with a hoarse voice, "You don't drink, Memphis?"

"I do," he says. "I drink coffee."

"Coffee at dinner?" Paulette says, taking another small sip of her margarita. "I'd never sleep again."

"Who says I want to?" he asks.

"Wow, this is some of the best chili I've ever had, Mar," Austin says—pointlessly shortening her name into a nick-name when her name is already so short—as he shovels a bite into his mouth before he's even seated. "Seriously."

"Well, don't sound so shocked," she teases, her cheeks tingeing pink. "You know who you're talking to, don't you?"

"She's the cookbook queen," Paulette says, fanning her hands toward Mara and pretending to fawn over her.

She's right. None of us should be shocked at Mara's love of cooking, or her ability to do it well. Though her account is mainly used to promote the books she's reading, she often shares recipes to pair with them or meals that were featured in the book. I've always said her food and photos deserve their own cookbooks.

I fill my bowl, sprinkling it with cheese and jalapeños before dropping in a dollop of sour cream and a handful of crackers. Mara waits until we've all gotten our bowls full to fill her own, piling it high with everything available. With the kitchen clean, Logan eventually joins us, and we begin to eat.

It's Austin who finally breaks the silence that has set in by saying, "So, I guess we should toast to our first night here. Our first weekend meeting each other, officially, for what I hope won't be the last time." He lifts the margarita in front of him, and we follow suit, stretching to tap our glasses together in the center of the table.

"And to Ethan for planning all of this," Mara says, somewhat sadly.

"Wish he could be here," I add before taking a sip of my drink.

"Here, here," Memphis chimes in, and I realize I've just implied I wish Ethan was here, which would mean Memphis wouldn't be. My eyes dart to him, and he taps his drink in the air toward me before taking another sip.

In his eyes, I catch a hint of something unrecognizable, and I can't tell whether or not I've offended him.

"Okay, so I thought of a game we can all play later," Austin says.

"Sounds ominous," Memphis mutters, taking a bite of his chili without looking his way.

"Bookish confessions." Austin holds up his hands like he's highlighting a marquee sign with the words printed on it. "Kind of like Never Have I Ever and Truth or Dare combined, but all book related. So, everyone confesses something on a slip of paper, we drop it in a bowl or hat or something, and then someone opens and reads each one, and we have to guess whose confession it is."

"What sort of confessions?" Logan asks, placing his spoon down in the bowl.

"Like...I dog-ear pages, or I always skip the sex scenes."

Paulette snorts. "Well, we all know that isn't me. I read those suckers twice." She holds up two fingers proudly.

"Yeah, you do!" Mara cries encouragingly, nodding as she claps her hands, mouth full.

"Really? Interesting. Any good ones to recommend?" Austin asks, resting his chin on his folded hands and studying Paulette, his ears red.

"Oh, honey. How much time do you have?" She laughs, pulling out her phone and opening a note before sliding it across the table toward Austin. "Here are my favorites."

I watch as Austin scrolls the list. And scrolls. And

scrolls. When he's done, he passes the phone back. "That's quite a list."

"I want to see it next!" Mara begs, wiggling her fingers toward the phone. Paulette passes it to her.

"What about you, Lena? Are you into sex scenes?" Memphis asks, fighting against a smirk as he takes a sip of his coffee.

I stare him down, my jaw locked as I respond. "I much prefer murder."

"Same," Logan agrees, but I can't bring myself to look away from Memphis. There's something playful in his eyes as he looks down, then glances back up at me for half a second, and I don't understand it. If he hates me so much, why is he being nice?

"Do any of you guys read romance?" Mara asks, staring at Austin as she slides the phone back to Paulette after snapping photos of her list.

"Not really," Austin says with a shrug.

"Me either," Logan agrees.

"Men," Mara groans. "Figures the people who could actually stand to learn a thing or two from the stories are the ones refusing to read them."

"Hey, I'll have you know there's nothing in those pages I need to learn, and I'm happy to prove it," Austin says in between bites with a warm smile. He locks eyes with Mara for several seconds, the table falling silent, and I can't help thinking of our conversation earlier. Mara might get her chance with Austin after all.

"My parents are super religious," Logan says, breaking the silence. "So, I wasn't allowed to read anything they deemed inappropriate. Romance. Magic. Books from the

Harry Potter series might as well have been *Satan's Guide to Getting Into Hell* in my house." He shakes his head with a laugh. "Anyway, so I started with The Hardy Boys as a kid and have pretty much stuck with mysteries ever since."

"Are you still close with your family?" Paulette asks.

"Eh, sort of. I mean, we don't agree on much anymore, but they're family, so what are you going to do?" He shrugs. "Anyway, I was a military brat, and we were always traveling, so I didn't have time to make many friends. They were all I had."

"No siblings?" I ask.

"Nope, just me." He gives a sad grin. "Lucky me."

"Military," Paulette muses. "That explains how neat you are. Did I see you lint rolling your shirt earlier?" She points her spoon at him, slinging a drop of tomato juice across the table.

He looks away. "Force of habit."

"Hey, no judgment," she says, hands up. "You could teach me a thing or two. I grew up in a house with four older brothers and a younger sister. It was a zoo. Still is, most days."

"Wow, six kids." Mara's eyes widen. "It's just me and my sister, and I think most days my parents were lucky to make it through the day. I can't imagine."

"It was fun, though. I loved my childhood." Paulette drains the last of her chili from her bowl, diving in for seconds. "And, you know, as far as my parents, I'm sure pot helped *a lot*." Everyone laughs as she refills her bowl, then sits back down in her chair. "Anyway, that game sounds like fun, Austin. Count me in."

"Me, too," I agree.

"Me three," says Logan.

When the meal is done, Mara and Logan get a break and head for their rooms while Austin and I clean up and put away the food, and Paulette does the dishes. Memphis also disappears, though I'm not sure where he went.

"So, Lena Beena, what do you think of the place? First impressions?" Austin asks, giving me a strange nickname as he peers at me and leans against the refrigerator door.

"It's nice." I fold up the bag of oyster crackers, searching in the drawers for a clip or clothespin to seal them up. "I mean, the town is a little too tiny for me. Next time, we definitely need to try visiting a city. I could use a night out downtown."

"Yes, girl!" Paulette cries, rocking her hips back and forth as if dancing to music no one else can hear. "I wanna go to a club!"

I chuckle.

"Noted. Well, *next time*, maybe we can plan it together." He shuffles closer to me—so close I catch the musky scent of his sweat. Austin is cute in the California-surfer sort of way. His curly, brown hair hangs down over his ears, and of the men here, he's the one I'm closest to. He reaches forward and tucks a piece of my hair behind my ear, running his teeth over his bottom lip.

Dating him, or even just sleeping with him, would be easy. But...I've done easy. My ex was easy. Being with him was so simple it made *not* being with him seem ridiculous. He was charming and handsome and friendly. Everyone who knew him loved him.

But eventually, the charm wore off, and I saw through it. And, by that point, it was too late. If nothing else came from the divorce, I've learned from my past mistakes, and I will never allow myself to repeat them.

Besides, Mara is obviously interested in him, and I would never do that to her.

I take a small step back. "Yeah. Maybe."

His face falls, the smile disappearing, but he recovers quickly. "Alright, awesome. Cool." His head bobs up and down as I grab a plastic clip from the drawer and close the crackers before shoving them into a mostly empty cabinet.

I grab an open bag of Starbursts and pull out a handful, unwrapping a yellow candy first. Force of habit. I always work my way from my least favorite food or flavor to my favorite when I'm eating anything, so the red candy in my hand will be the last one I eat.

"Do you guys want another drink?" Austin asks. "I was thinking of staying up for a while. I think everyone else might be down for the night."

"I'm always okay with a drink," Paulette says, shutting off the water and grabbing a towel to dry her hands. "What about you, Lena? You in?"

I wave a hand at them with a yawn, only then realizing just how tired I am. "Nah. I think I'm going to go to bed. The flight took it out of me. I'll see you both in the morning."

"You sure?" she asks.

"Mm-hmm. Positive. Sorry, I'm boring." I draw in one side of my mouth.

"Hey, that's okay," Austin says genuinely. "It doesn't make you boring. I'm tired, too. I just have this condition where I'm chronically incapable of making wise choices."

It takes me a moment to realize what he's said, but once I do, I release a loud laugh. "Oh my god."

He flashes me a wide smile and pats my back. "Seriously. We have plenty of other nights to all hang out. Tomorrow we'll play the game I mentioned. You just go and get some rest."

"Yeah," Paulette agrees, tossing the wet towel on the counter. "We'll see you in the morning."

"Okay, good night, you guys."

"Good night," Austin calls as he heads to the fridge, already discussing the drink options with Paulette.

With the last of the food put away, I disappear down the hall and up the stairs, ready to pass out from exhaustion.

CHAPTER FIVE

When I wake the next morning, the house is quiet. I've always been an early riser, so I'm surprised to see the sun is already up. It must be after six.

After brushing my teeth, washing my face, and changing into warmer clothes, I slip downstairs and make myself a cup of coffee. I pour in the oat milk Mara bought and add a dash of cinnamon, plus spoonfuls of stevia to make it just right.

Next, I slip out of the kitchen and onto the back porch, where there's a set of wicker rocking chairs with a small wooden table in between them. I sit down, inhaling a deep breath and closing my eyes.

For all my hatred of small towns, I can't help but understand the appeal in this moment. The peace and quiet I could never find in the city. The stillness of it all. It's sort of enchanting in its own way.

Before I can appreciate it too much, the silence is interrupted by the slamming of a door. I jolt and tear my eyes open, searching around for the source of the sound.

When I find it, I go still. Two people—a man and a woman—are stopped in the middle of the porch at the house next door. Midforties, I'd say. Moderately attractive, albeit plain.

She has sleek, shoulder-length, dark-brown hair and blunt bangs, and is wearing an all-white tracksuit. The man next to her has black hair that falls to his back in curls. His chin and cheeks are covered in dark facial hair with crisp, clean lines that keep him from looking scraggly. She's carrying something—a box of items I can't see—and they're having a discussion, their hushed tones silenced by the wind and distance between us.

I sink into my chair farther, hoping to remain unnoticed from where I sit. Hidden in plain sight.

The man leans closer to her, saying something with a stern expression, and she balks, leaning back with brows drawn down. She shakes her head, and he holds out his hands, trying to take the box from her.

Creeeeaak.

I jerk my head toward the sound, realizing all at once my cover has been blown. Memphis stands in the doorway with a mug of coffee in his hands and a strange look on his face. He doesn't seem to notice the neighbors.

Releasing the screen door, he lets it shut the rest of the way, slamming closed. "I didn't know anyone was out here. Mind the company?"

I avert my attention back toward the neighbors, checking without hope to see if it's possible they didn't hear us and don't realize I've been spying on them.

To my mortification, I find them both staring at us

from across the lawn. I lift a hand and wave awkwardly as Memphis moves toward the railing.

"Morning," he calls, waving.

I lift my cup, taking a drink and looking away, staring hard in any direction but theirs as if to say I've just been sitting out here minding my own business and not at all watching them.

They give us forced smiles, then quickly disappear inside their house, shutting the door without a look back.

"Neighborly," he mutters, sipping his coffee.

"Gotta love that small-town charm," I muse, narrowing my eyes at him. "What are you doing out here? Why are you up so early?"

"My alarm goes off at six," he says between sips of coffee. "Just took a shower and needed breakfast." He lifts the mug, then eyes me. "I wasn't aware this was early."

As the wind picks up, making music with the wind chime hanging from the edge of the porch, I pull my legs up into the seat with me, tucking my feet under myself to keep them warm. Even in fuzzy socks, they're practically icicles. "We're on vacation. Everyone else is still asleep."

"Not you." He doesn't bother looking at me as he says it.

"I always wake up early."

"Me, too." His shoulder lifts with a shrug.

"You just said you have to set an alarm. I wake up without one."

"You want a prize?" he snips, looking my way with a hint of humor in his voice.

"I'm just saying, it's vacation. If I could sleep in, I

would in a heartbeat. Why aren't you sleeping in if you can?"

"I still have stuff to do for the store. Inventory, emails."

I eye him, shocked. "You're working? But...you have employees."

"Yeah, well, I like to be hands-on with stuff. I guess I'm a bit of a control freak."

I bite my tongue to keep from saying that I've noticed.

Memphis sinks down in the rocking chair next to me with a sigh, adjusting the flannel shirt he's wearing. He's quiet for a while before he says, "The store was important to my parents. And, now it's mine."

With just those words, I get it. "And you don't want to fail."

He looks away without a word.

"Is that why you didn't hire me? Because I failed your test, and you think I'd manage to screw something up?"

He scowls. "Is that what you think?"

"I know the right answer to your question was *Of Mice and Men*."

"How could you know that?"

I stare at him without giving an answer, but he seems to get it anyway.

"Mary." He rolls his eyes.

I nod. "How can you honestly expect anyone to know that? Just tell us you want us to recommend it, and we will."

"It's not about the book," he says with a long sigh. "Not really. I just...I don't know. Have you ever lost anyone?"

55

"Well, that's a big question for six thirty in the morning."

"Answer it."

"I just went through a divorce, so I lost someone in that sense. Yeah. But, no, both of my parents and all four grand-parents are still alive. I lost a great-aunt when I was younger, but I know it's not the same."

"I'm sorry about the divorce," he says, his dark eyes dancing between mine. "I didn't know."

"Yeah, well, on the list of my accomplishments I like to brag about, it falls pretty low."

The joke falls flat as he stares at me like something is sitting on the tip of his tongue, begging to be said. "Ever since I lost my parents, I look for pieces of them. Signs they're still...I don't know, with me or whatever. I ask the question because I think I'm waiting for the perfect person to give me the right answer..." He looks down, burying his face in his palm.

"To let you know your dad's still here." In a strange way, I guess it makes sense.

"It's stupid, I fully realize that. But, some days, it's all I have."

"You have the store. That's all the proof you need that they're still with you." Awkwardly, I lift my hand and place it on his shoulder.

He looks over at it as if I've burned him, then looks up at me, our eyes locking. For several seconds, nothing happens. We just stare at each other, breathing, existing. I can't form rational thoughts. Can't form any thoughts, really.

I don't understand what's happening.

He clears his throat, and I rip my hand away from him. *Why the hell did I do that?*

I open my mouth, searching for something—*anything* —to say. "I, um—"

"I shouldn't have walked out of the interview in the way I did. I'm sorry." He blurts the words out as if they've been burning his tongue.

"Thank you." I give him a small smile and stare down into my mug. "For the record, I wish I could've gotten the answer right."

He looks away. "Yeah, well, for the record, your wrong answer isn't why I didn't hire you."

The words wash over me. "What do you mean?"

He stands, crossing the porch to lean against the railing again, his back to me. "Look, I'm going to say this, and then we're never going to speak about it again, okay?"

"What?"

"Do we have a deal?"

"Yeah, sure. I guess."

He draws in a long inhale. My entire body is on pins and needles as I await his next words.

"I don't hire people I'm attracted to."

"Wha—"

He turns around, resting against the railing, and shoves one hand into the pocket of his jeans. I can't bear to meet his eyes, and yet, I can't look away. "That's why I didn't hire you. Maybe that's a terrible thing to say. You could probably sue me or something, but it's the truth, so...there you go. It just hasn't worked out for me in the past, and I have a rule about it now."

My cheeks must be the color of tomatoes, as hot as they feel. "Okay."

"Okay?" he asks, moving back to his seat and sitting down. "We good?"

"Yep." I nod.

"Okay. Cool."

I expect to find my mind racing with questions, but instead, it's eerily silent, as if I can't comprehend what's just happened.

"I'm sorry if me being here has made this weekend awkward for you."

"Surprisingly, it hasn't." I study him, but he still isn't looking at me. "Is it... I mean, is it awkward for you? What with you being wildly attracted to me and all that?"

He rolls his eyes and puffs a playful breath out his nose, cracking a smile. "I knew I shouldn't have said anything."

"I'm just saying."

"*Wildly* is a bit of a stretch. Mildly, maybe."

"Mm-hmm." I lift the cup to my lips, staring at him over the rim. "Is that all you ever drink?" I tease, looking at the coffee in his mug.

"What?"

"I just realized I don't think I've ever seen you drink anything besides coffee. At the store... Even at dinner last night. Everyone had the margaritas Mara made, but not you. It's always coffee."

He turns to me with a wry grin. "You stalking me or something, Ortega?"

"Please," I scoff. "I was invited to this place first, remember? If anyone's stalking anyone, it's you stalking me. Clearly because—"

"If you say it's because I'm attracted to you one more time—"

"You should've never given me the ammunition."

"I'm starting to realize that." He flexes his jaw, his eyes drilling into mine, then drags a hand over his cheek. "Look, for the record, I didn't know you'd be here. Austin didn't tell me anything about who was coming when he invited me."

"That was who you were talking to during my interview?"

He nods. "It was. I was trying to find every excuse not to come, but he guilted me into it."

I look down, toying with a piece of lint on my sweater. The wind picks up, the icy breeze hitting me square in the face. On it, I catch a hint of smoke and hear the leaves blowing on the ground around the porch. It's every bit a fall morning here—crisp and cool and nearly completely silent. You could lose yourself in it if you tried. I take another sip of my drink, letting the warmth fill me. "I can't believe you guys are friends."

"Why?" He fiddles with a button on his flannel absent-mindedly, watching me. As I try to come up with an answer, a way to put my scrambled thoughts into words, a few more leaves fall from the nearly bare tree next to the porch.

"I don't know. I guess it's just that you're so different."

His hand drops to his lap. "Meaning?"

I focus my attention on him. "He's...fun. I don't know. Carefree."

"And I'm not." He nods, looking away.

My heart drops, and I run a hand over the leg of my

sweatpants, suddenly even colder than I was before. "I didn't say that. I didn't mean—"

"I know what you meant." His tone is clipped, his voice icy. Suddenly, he's refusing to look my way. "Trust me, I'm not offended. I realize I'm nothing like Austin. Wild and free and easy... I'm never going to be any of those things."

Easy. The word spills out of his mouth as if he read my thoughts last night. "So, if you'd known I'd be here, you wouldn't have come?"

He looks at me then, stares my way with a heavy bitterness in his expression, and I can't tell if he's angry at me or himself. "I don't know, Lena. All I know is...I didn't mean to come across as rude during our interview, despite having my reasons. I should've handled it better. And I didn't mean to overstep by being here, either."

I tilt my head to the side. "Is that another apology?"

He lifts his hand, opening his mouth, then drops his palm to his knee, puffing out a breath from his nose. "It's a clarification. I don't want there to be any hard feelings between us."

I lick my dry lips. They're beginning to get chapped from this cold air, but I refuse to leave right now. "Well, thank you for clarifying, then."

"Are there?" he presses, swirling the coffee around in his mug. "Hard feelings?"

"Not on my end," I say simply, brushing hair back from my face when the wind picks up again.

"Good." If he's pleased, he shows no signs of it. If anything, he looks angrier than before.

"Good," I repeat. "So, is that the only reason you set your alarm to wake up early? To do things for the store?"

He nods, draining more of the liquid from his mug. "I like to have my responsibilities handled before the day sets in. That way there's room for things to fall apart."

"That's probably a smart way to look at it, but also a pessimistic one."

He gives a wry grin with a faraway look in his eyes. "A realistic one, more like it."

"Do things frequently fall apart for you, then?" I ask, trying and failing to make a joke that clearly doesn't land.

He swallows and turns his head to look at the house next door. "My family didn't have very much when I was growing up. Just the store and our apartment. We struggled most of my life. My parents taught me the value of hard work. They were at the store from five in the morning until well after midnight each night, making sure everything was perfect, cleaning, stocking shelves, placing orders, and doing whatever else needed to be done. They couldn't afford to hire employees to help for the longest time. And, even once they could, it was all on them, always."

He pauses for so long I think he's done talking. When I open my mouth to respond—though I have no idea what I'll be saying—he goes on, "And when they died last year, two months apart from two completely separate, random things, it all fell on me. I always knew the store would be mine someday, but I wasn't ready. I'm still not ready. And I know if it doesn't work out, if I fail, I'll have screwed up their entire legacy."

He glances down. "So that's why the coffee and the early alarm. That's why I couldn't chance hiring you just to do something stupid and let my feelings get involved and screw everything up. I don't have luxury of sleeping in or letting my emotions make decisions for me because everything my parents worked for is firmly on my shoulders. I don't have time for vacations, for...for any of this..."

"That's a lot of pressure," I say gently. I can't imagine if I didn't have my parents to fall back on after my divorce. My safety net. If they hadn't offered up their spare room, I'm not sure what would've happened to me. Though it's been my greatest embarrassment, I'm incredibly thankful it was an option.

"Yeah, well...it is what it is. I came because Austin is a friend, and he said you guys wouldn't be able to come without splitting the cost six ways. He's had a rough few years. He gets losing parents the way most people our age don't, so...here I am. But that doesn't make it easy."

"You deserve a break, though, Memphis. And Mary seems like she has things under control. She's amazing."

A small smile plays on his lips. "Yeah, well, she was one of the few employees my parents ever hired and probably the best thing they ever did for the store. So..." His eyes land on me, full of something I can't read. "Whoever I hire first has to stack up."

I try to ignore the sting of his words, forcing a joke. "And be wildly unattractive."

"That too," he says. "I just need someone to help me get this right. It wasn't personal, and I'm sure you'd be great."

"Just these damn good looks." My voice cracks as I try to fake confidence I don't have. I don't understand why I suddenly feel like crying. I don't know what to say to that or how not being right because of the way I look could be less personal, but I don't have to dwell on it, because as I'm searching for a response, I hear heavy footsteps heading our way from inside the house. Then the door opens and Mara and Austin are standing there, their upper arms touching in a way that feels intimate.

Mara grins at Austin, then at me. When her eyes land on Memphis, one brow quirks up, and she returns her attention to me. "Well, good morning. What an interesting little situation we have here." It's impossible that Memphis could miss the mischievous tone of her voice or what she's hinting at. Her dark hair has been pulled back in a loose ponytail, face makeup free aside from a shine to her lips that must be lip balm.

"I could say the same thing," I tease, eyeing her and Austin.

She rolls her eyes, brushing a stray strand of hair from her mouth as it fights to cling to the sticky balm on her lips. "Well, I had to recruit Austin to help me look for my best friend because I thought she'd gone missing. I checked your room and saw you weren't there. We were very concerned." Her lips pinch with a smile. "It was a very serious mission, wasn't it, Austin?"

She tilts her head toward him, and he winks at me. "Oh, very serious."

"Well, mission accomplished. You found me in my super-secret hiding spot," I tease.

"That's because we're great spies." Mara pats Austin's shoulder.

"I don't think great spies announce that they're spies," Memphis points out under his breath.

Mara either didn't hear him or chooses to ignore him as she steps around Austin, moving toward me. "Why are you out here, for real? Is everything okay? Why are you even up this early?"

I lift the coffee mug in answer. "I couldn't sleep. So... breakfast."

"Well, we were thinking we could go on a trip today," Austin says with a grin. "Mara found a small, local bookstore a town away, and we can get more groceries while we're there, too."

"Sounds like a plan," I say.

Memphis stands and walks inside, and I know we're both going to have to pretend none of the heavy stuff that just went on between us ever happened.

"You sure you're okay?" Mara asks, holding out a hand. "Was he bothering you?"

"No, I'm fine. We were just talking." I slide my hand into hers, and she squeezes it, resting her head on my shoulder briefly.

"Okay." She practically sings the word. "If you're sure. Are you ready for an adventure, then?"

Ready as I'll ever be. "Let's go."

CHAPTER SIX

Two hours later, the rideshare Austin booked drops us off in a town thirty minutes from ours. The city is small, but there's a walkable downtown with a bookstore, coffee shop, and a few markets.

We hit the bookstore first, moving in a cloud of determination for the thrillers. To my surprise, even Memphis joins us, in a visibly better mood than before.

I choose two books I've been meaning to read and one that I'm nearly positive I don't already own, tucking them under my arm as I peruse the rest of the aisles.

I could spend hours inside bookstores, never growing tired of being among the pages. It's strange, but there's a peace in them that I don't find anywhere else. Shelves of possibilities. Of lives yet to be lived. Of loves yet to fall into. Terror yet to be experienced.

Mara has a single book tucked under her arm when she approaches me, ready to compare. "Oh, that one looks dark." She points to the top book in my stack, a Mari

Morgan novel everyone's been raving about. "Have you read it yet?"

"Not yet, but it's been on my list for a while. What'd you get?"

"Find anything good, ladies?" Austin asks, approaching the table we're standing next to before Mara can show me the book she chose. He's holding a book by an author named Tennessee Rivers and a pair of socks designed to look like crossword puzzles, wagging them around in front of him. "This place is pretty cool."

"Check it out!" Paulette says, coming up behind me. She's wearing thick eyeliner and a T-shirt with an opossum sporting a cowboy hat next to the words, **Grant me the serenity to accept the vibes that aren't rootin' tootin'.** In her hand, she's holding a collection of Edgar Allen Poe stories. "They have a whole section in the back that's forty percent off. Did you see?"

"What?" Logan asks, darting toward the discounted books section.

Mara turns to join him, but before I can follow, Memphis approaches me.

"Hey. Can I ask you something?"

My chest tightens as I glance up at him. I can still feel Mara's watchful gaze as she waits to see what I'm going to do. Eventually, I nod. "Uh, sure." I glance over at her. "Go ahead. I'll catch up with you guys."

She hesitates. "You sure?"

"Yeah, go ahead. I'll be right there."

Once she's gone, I return my attention to Memphis. "So? What's up?"

He puffs out the question on a breath. "What do you think of this place?"

"Huh?" That wasn't what I was expecting.

"Like, what do you think they're doing right?"

I look around then back at him. "Wait, are you doing *market research* right now?"

He grasps the three books he's holding in front of his stomach, squaring his stance. "I can't help it. They're set up very differently than we are, and it has my mind going. I wonder which setup you prefer. There may be things they're doing here that I could incorporate into my store."

"Your store is fine, Memphis. You really don't know how to relax, do you?"

"I shopped," he says defensively, lifting the three books in his arms as proof.

I study them. "Hmm... Two out of three are independent authors. Let me guess...you don't carry them in your store and are going to see if you should?"

His face falls. "Fine. I'm researching. Sue me."

I laugh. "Well, for the record, I like the way your store is set up, but I do appreciate the options here. And the way each section is labeled. So many independent bookstores just have a fiction section, but I like when they're labeled by specific genre. It helps narrow it down so there's a better chance I'll find what I'm looking for."

"Noted," he says, pulling out his phone and quite literally jotting down the note. "Genre...labels." He slips the phone back into his pocket with a nod. "Give me a week, and it's done."

"Okay, now, for ten seconds, let's pretend you aren't a

hardworking business owner and just shop for cheap books. What do you say?"

He scowls but follows me to the back of the store where our group has already picked through the selection of discounts.

"Lena, come look at what I found," Mara calls, holding out her hand. I join her, sifting through the piles. "What was that about?" she whispers, leaning closer to me while still pretending to shop.

"Nothing. He was just asking about how this store compares to his."

"You two certainly seem to be getting chummy," she says with a sly grin.

"He's not so bad." As I say it, I shoot a glance across the table of books, watching as a small smile forms on Memphis's lips, though he isn't looking my way. I can't help wondering if he's listening in, though we're being quiet.

As if he senses me staring, his eyes lift to find mine, though he doesn't move his head.

Immediately, I look away, feeling my cheeks flush with heat.

"What about you and Austin?" I nod my head in his direction.

"Baby steps," she says simply, shrugging one shoulder. "But I'm wearing him down slowly."

"He'd be an idiot for letting you get away."

She bumps my arm with hers and tosses a bit of hair over her shoulder. "Oh, trust me, I know."

Once we're done, we head for the checkout, where an

older woman with gray hair braided down her back greets us.

"Wow," she says with a bright little giggle. "You kids certainly have your hands full. Did you find everything you were looking for?"

"And then some," I joke. "You have such good deals on your books."

She sighs, scanning my books and slipping them into a paper bag. "Yes, well, I'm sad to say I'm having to close the shop permanently. So, I'm slowly marking everything down."

My heart sinks. "Oh. I'm so sorry. I didn't realize."

"Well, you know how things are around here." One side of her cheek draws in.

"Small towns are tough," I agree. "We're actually not from here. We're just in town for a visit."

"Oh." She eyes us somewhat suspiciously. I pay for my order and step back so Memphis can move forward and begin checking out. "Family in town?"

"No, it's kind of a strange story, actually. A friend of ours found a vacation rental in Fulfield and thought it would be a good place for all of us to get away," Austin explains.

"Well, it certainly is a place to get away. Fulfield's even quieter than we are. I can't imagine there's much for you youngins to do there."

After Memphis pays for his, Mara walks forward. "We went down to the river yesterday," she says. "It's so beautiful."

The woman, whose name tag introduces her as Bertie,

makes a soft *hmph* noise and neither agrees nor disagrees. "How long are you in town?"

"Just the weekend," I tell her as Mara pays and moves back to make room for Paulette. "We head back home Sunday."

"Well, just take care of yourselves, okay? This may be a sleepy little small town, but we've got our problems just like everywhere else." She's quiet for a long while, leaving us with that ominous message.

Once we've all checked out and are preparing to leave, she adds, "Come back and see me anytime while you're here, okay? It's nice to have some friendly faces in town."

"Will do," Austin calls, and we all wave and say our goodbyes.

Outside the store, Mara rushes to keep up with Austin, walking beside him as she and Paulette laugh over something I can't hear. Memphis slows his pace, remaining with me at the back of the group and letting everyone else get ahead of us. We walk side by side for several moments, neither of us saying anything, just taking in the sunny but cold day and listening to the rustle of our bags in the wind. He seems to have something on his mind, but I'm almost afraid to ask what it is.

"Look, don't make this weird, but I found something for you," he says, all in one breath like he's been waiting to say the words.

"What?"

He reaches inside his bag and pulls out a copy of the latest Arlie Montgomery novel, and I could swear my heart stalls.

"How did you..."

"You picked it up twice while we were in there and kept putting it back. I just figured you should have it." He nudges it toward me again until I take it.

"Memphis, this is really nice. Thank you."

"It's not a big deal." He sniffles and looks straight ahead. "Consider it my apology for not hiring you."

I laugh and place the book in my bag. "Well, then, consider this my apology for getting your answer wrong." I pull out the special edition hardbound copy of *Of Mice and Men*.

He stares at it with wide eyes, turning it over in his hands. "Where did you find this?"

"It was in the discounted section. I thought you'd like to have it."

He looks up at me with a stoic expression, mouth dropped open but no words coming out. Eventually, he clears his throat. "Thank you. Seriously. This is... You didn't have to do this."

"Don't mention it." I wave him off.

Eventually, he places the book in his bag, but neither of us makes an effort to pick up the pace and remain with the group. Instead, we stay back in comfortable silence, taking turns pretending not to glance at each other.

Whatever is happening here is weird and uncomfortable, yet it's the most comfortable thing I've ever felt. I both dislike and am enamored with Memphis in equal measure.

As we walk, his arm brushes mine a few more times than necessary, and each time, I feel a little twinge somewhere deep inside my chest.

It's midafternoon before we get back to the house, our stomachs full of pastries and coffee from the local coffee shop and bags full of groceries and books.

We've decided to make a full spread for dinner. Logan and Memphis are going to cook steak and vegetables while Mara, Paulette, and I prepare the drinks—cranberry orange whiskey sours—and Austin is on salad duty.

While we work, Logan turns on the audiobook he just got from his library, one we all agree we've been waiting to read. We work in silence, zoning out to the narrator's smooth voice, the sizzling of the meat in Memphis's skillet, and the rhythmic *chop, chop, chop* of Austin's knife against the wooden cutting board as he slices and dices the vegetables for our salad.

"So, I was thinking we should do a collab," Paulette tells Mara and me, keeping her voice low. "Like the three of us review the same book in a post and maybe do a giveaway. We could do a different book for each of our pages and a giveaway for each."

"Oooh," Mara sings. She bumps Paulette's hip with hers, then mine. "I am *in*. That sounds like fun."

"Maybe we could do it with books we bought here, so we could take a photo of the three of us with each book. Like a group photo," I add.

"Yes, that's smart!" Mara claps me on the back. "I love it."

"I'd talked to Ethan about doing that before," I say. "So, I can't take all the credit for it. We were planning to take a few photos together this weekend with books we've both loved and share them throughout the year."

"You two are pretty close, aren't you?" Mara asks,

looking at me with a sly grin. "Memphis is going to be *jealous.*"

"*Shhh!*" At the mention of him, I look up to find his eyes on me from across the room. I know he couldn't possibly have heard her, but the idea sends a chill over me. "Don't be silly. No one is jealous."

Paulette and Mara exchange knowing glances, their lips pursed.

"*Anyway,*" I go on, "yes, we're close. I mean, same as the rest of us. I was looking forward to finally getting to meet him."

She lifts her eyebrows playfully. "*Meet* him, hm?"

"M-e-*a*-t, maybe," Paulette adds with a cackle, and Mara nudges her with an approving look.

"Yeah, she was." She nods her head, rocking her hips toward the table like she'd done upstairs yesterday about Memphis.

I groan. "Shut up, you two. You're the worst."

"You ladies seem like you're up to no good over there," Austin says, drawing our attention to him.

"We were just talking about Ethan," Paulette tells him quickly.

"Yeah, just saying how sad it is that he couldn't make it," I add before she can say anything more humiliating.

"He mentioned that the funeral is today, so he might try to stop by Saturday night if he's feeling up to it, but I don't really expect him to make it. I remember how crazy my grandmother's funeral was, and my parents' funerals too. There was no way I was up for traveling immediately after," Austin says, returning to chopping a stalk of celery.

"Where would he stay?" Logan asks. "All of the rooms are full."

Austin shrugs. "Couch, I guess."

Mara's stare burns into me, and when I look over, she nudges her tongue into her cheek. "He could stay in Lena's room," she offers too loudly.

I shove into her playfully. "Hush."

"Aww, we can't have little ole Lena giving up her bed," Austin says. "I'll be a gentleman and let him have mine. I don't mind crashing on the couch." He eyes me. "Unless you were planning to share it with him?"

BANG.

Every head in the room turns toward where Memphis is preparing the steaks. He quickly picks up the jar of seasoning he dropped on the stove without a look in our direction. "Sorry. Slipped out of my hand."

Mara's gaze darts my way, and I suddenly realize, with all this talk about Ethan, I still haven't heard back from him. I pull out my phone and check my text messages, then social media. I open his profile to see he hasn't posted anything since last week, which makes sense with the funeral and everything, but it still worries me. I hope he's doing okay, that he knows I'm here if he needs to talk.

"Everything okay?" Paulette asks, studying me.

"Yeah, I just...I sent him a message yesterday and haven't heard back."

"I'm sure he's just busy," she says, her eyes soft and sympathetic, as if she suspects—as I do—that I'm being blown off. "Like Austin said, funeral weekends are a lot."

"Yeah. Right. No, of course. I know. I just wanted to

check on him. He hasn't posted online in a few days, so I'm sure he's just been off his phone in general."

"He knows you care." Mara pets my arm gently with a lopsided smile. "That's what matters. He'll see it when he gets a chance. And, in the meantime, we're having..." She busts into a loud rendition of that "The Time of My Life" song I only know from the *Dirty Dancing* movie my parents love so much.

Logan pauses the audiobook when Paulette joins in on the song, and soon, the two of them are dancing around the room using wooden spoons as microphones to perform while Austin, Memphis, Logan, and I watch and cheer for them. Er, at least Austin and I cheer for them. Logan mostly nervously follows them, cleaning up spills as they bump into Austin's chopping board, a stack of books, and my open bag of Starbursts from last night. Next to me, Memphis just chuckles to himself and shakes his head.

When Memphis finishes with the steaks, we carry the food and drinks to the table.

I return to the kitchen to get the plates and silverware and find Logan sweeping up any food we dropped while cooking. "Need any help with that?"

He shakes his head, squatting down to sweep the scraps into the dustpan. "I've got it."

"You know you don't have to do that, right? We should all be pitching in more." I tap my fingers on the countertop, feeling guilty. "It's your vacation, too."

"I don't mind." He stands up, turning to empty the dustpan into the trash can. "I relax easier when there's not a mess. It's my problem, not yours. I know everyone's only having fun. I just hope you all don't find me annoying about it."

I reach up and open a cabinet, grabbing a stack of plates. "Not at all. Everyone has their quirks. As long as you don't think we're lazy."

He smiles and opens his mouth, prepared to say something, when I hear the sound of a door slamming outside.

"What was that?"

I move around to the back door and ease outside as he heads to put the broom away. Curious for another peek at our peculiar neighbors, I step farther out onto the porch and spot them standing next to the black sedan in the driveway.

Their foreheads are pressed together in what looks like a loving embrace from a distance, but upon closer inspection, it appears threatening.

The way he's staring at her is intense. His jaw is tight; his grip on her arms is so angry I can see the white halo surrounding his fingerprints from here.

"Everything okay?" Memphis asks, surprising me by appearing in the doorway.

This time, I'm grateful when the neighbors hear us and immediately break apart. They look over at us, and I don't bother to wave. I want him to know I saw what just happened.

Want her to know.

They both turn and rush inside without another glance in our direction.

"I think I just caught them in the middle of a fight," I say softly, keeping my voice low.

Memphis's dark brows draw down. "Yeah?"

"I don't like him."

He puts a hand on my back, ushering me inside. "Do we need to call the police or something? Was it physical?"

I swallow, unsure of what to say. *No, he didn't hurt her, but would he have if we hadn't interrupted?* I don't want to be the kind of person who sits back and observes and never takes action. If she's in danger, I want to help. But I also can't help fearing getting involved if he is dangerous, or even if he's not.

If I call the police and they both deny anything happened, I could be putting a target on my head. Perhaps I'll call after we leave. It's just two more days.

"No, I don't think so."

"Let's go eat," he says, his eyes still on the neighbor's house. "Food's getting cold."

CHAPTER SEVEN

Dinner is mostly uneventful. Then again, I tune out most of the conversation, my head wrapped up in what I saw outside. I can't shake the feeling that the man next door might be dangerous, can't shake the guilt over doing nothing about it.

Memphis keeps looking over at me, giving his head a little dip whenever I meet his eyes as if to say "Are you alright?" Each time, I nod and pretend I am, but I don't think I'm fooling him.

When we finish eating, Logan pulls a bottle of wine from the fridge while Mara gets the glasses down.

"I was thinking we could play that game," Austin tells us, brushing his hair back from his face. "If everyone's feeling up to it."

"The Bookish Confessions one?" Mara asks, spinning around to look at him.

"Yeah."

"Sounds fun to me," Logan says, unscrewing the top from the wine and pouring himself a glass before passing the bottle around.

"Cool. I'll go find some paper and pens," Austin says, darting from the room.

"I think I saw some in the living room next to the TV," Paulette shouts after him, cupping her hands around her mouth so the sound carries further.

Memphis crosses the room to the coffee pot and pours himself a fresh cup, adding cream from the fridge. When he starts to walk away, I call after him without thinking, "Aren't you playing?"

He stops in his tracks, his eyes warming when he meets mine. "I have emails to catch up on."

"You aren't going to play?" Paulette cries as if utterly appalled.

"You have to play!" Mara says, crossing the room and taking his arm. "Come on. Doesn't he have to play, Lena?"

He looks at me, and I tilt my head sideways, asking without asking.

"Fine," he says, sliding his arm out of hers with a laugh. "I'll play."

"Yes!" She celebrates with a victory leap in the air, dragging her arm down with her elbow bent.

"I found them." Austin races into the room, out of breath, with a handful of pens and a notebook.

In the living room, we find our seats. I sit on the couch next to Mara, with Memphis on the floor next to the end of the couch. Paulette and Logan are in two of the wingback chairs in front of the window, and Austin sits on the floor to Mara's left, so we form a circle.

As he explains the rules of the game again, he tears out

slips of paper for everyone, passing the paper and pens around.

"I want the glittery one," Mara says when he hands her a plain ballpoint pen, swapping it out for the glittery purple pen in his hand.

"No." He takes it back.

"Hey!" she cries, trying to grab it from his hand.

"No. You can't use a pen that's recognizable. Everyone has to use these same ones. That way no one knows who wrote what." He hands her the first pen back, then drops the glitter one onto the coffee table next to one that doesn't work.

Once everyone has their papers and fully understands the rules, Austin leaves the room and returns a few moments later with an orange plastic serving bowl from the kitchen.

"Okay, here we go. So, write your bookish confession down, make sure no one sees you do it, fold it in half twice, and then drop it in the bowl."

He places the bowl onto the coffee table and sits down on the ground, grabbing a book from one of the stacks on the floor to lay his paper on.

"Oh! Hand me one?" Mara asks, holding out her hand.

"Me too," Memphis agrees.

Soon, we all have books in our hands and begin to write.

I try to think as the room goes quiet, filled with only the sound of Paulette tapping her pen against the back of her book rhythmically and the scratching of Logan's pen across his page.

I'm not sure what to write. I *do* dog-ear pages, which

was an example Austin gave, but now it feels too generic of a response. Next to me, Memphis and Mara have both begun to write.

"Don't make it complicated," Austin says, and when I look up, I realize he's looking at me. "It's just for fun."

I look down, deciding on my confession finally, and scribble it on the page. When I'm done, I fold it twice and drop it in the bowl.

With everyone's confession written down, Austin shakes it up. "Who wants to read them?"

"You go ahead," Mara tells him, scooting forward in her seat, arms folded across her knees.

I take a sip of my wine as he pulls the first paper out and unfolds it. His eyes widen.

"Oh, ho, ho. Wow. Okay, we're starting off with a bang. This one says, 'I prefer to read books by male authors.'" He drops the paper down to his lap and stares around. "If anyone confesses to that, I think you'll want to sleep with one eye open tonight."

My gaze falls to Memphis. But, if he's guilty, he's doing a good job faking it. In fact, everyone is. Every eye in the room is looking at everyone else.

"Any guesses who said it?" No one says anything for a long time, so Austin drops the paper onto the floor and digs for the next one. "Okay, then. Let's see." He pulls out the next paper and unfolds it slowly. "'When I'm reading a book and there's a name that's hard to pronounce,'" he reads, "'I just make something up in my head and roll with that. It's usually way off.'" He chuckles. "That's gotta be Paulette."

She throws her head back with a laugh, a hand in the air. "Guilty as charged."

"Okay, awesome. Next." He pulls out the next slip of paper, moving faster this time. "'If I really like a book, I'll buy it in paperback, ebook, and audio.'" He places the paper down, looking at me.

"Not me," I say quickly. "I mean, for my favorites, sure, but that's not my confession." I look at Mara, who shakes her head.

"Oh, come on," he says. "Whose is it, then? It's called Bookish Confessions. You have to actually confess." He checks with Logan and Memphis, but neither of them admit to the confession.

"Fine," he says with a playful sigh. "For the record, I do that, too. Anyone else do Paulette's thing or this one?"

There's a murmur of agreement before he goes on to the next confession.

"'I...'" He pauses. "Oh, this is interesting. 'I give up on books at any point if I've lost interest, whether that's chapter one or the second-to-last chapter.'" His brows bounce up as he laughs. "Oh, that's controversial."

That's my confession, but going along with the theme of not claiming it, I keep my hand in my lap.

"Logan, I can totally see that being you," Paulette says, pointing at him.

He shakes his head, hands up. "Nope, not me. I have to finish the books I start, even if I hate them."

"Why waste your time on books you don't like?" Memphis asks, scowling.

"How can you know you don't like them in the first

chapter?" Paulette asks with her voice raised, leaning forward dramatically.

"You just do," he says, shaking his head.

"Well, that one's clearly Memphis." Austin tosses it aside. "Cool. Next."

Memphis doesn't deny it, though we both know it's not him, as Austin pulls out the next one. He chuckles to himself. "This one says, 'When I read a book I don't like, I automatically go and look up the bad reviews on it to find community in my hatred.'"

To that, we all laugh.

"Such a good one," Paulette says. "I do the same."

"Me, too." I grin over my guilty pleasure. I had no idea anyone else did that.

"Monsters," Austin says, his mouth dropped open with a feign of shock. "Okay, last one." He tosses the paper aside and lifts the last one out of the bowl. "'If I buy a hardcover and it has a dust jacket, I immediately throw it out.'"

"Oh, same!" Logan cries, hand in the air.

Austin looks up, but I notice his eyes don't travel the room like usual, and when he says, "Anyone want to claim it?" It's only half convincing. "Okay, cool. Game over. Should we go another round?" He picks up his pen and clicks it.

"I will, but I need more wine," Paulette replies, standing from her seat and bounding across the room. She returns a few moments later and refills her glass, then Mara's, Austin's, and Logan's. When she comes to me, I still have half a glass, so I shake my head, and she places the bottle onto the table next to me. "It's there when you want it."

For the next round, everyone seems to write down their

answers more quickly, and before I know it, Austin is drawing the first slip of paper out of the bowl.

"Okay." He draws in a long inhale. "'I often find myself making the faces the characters in the books are making.'"

I laugh, leaning back in my seat because, once again, it's something I do, too.

"Anyone claiming it?" He pauses. "Any guesses?"

It's Memphis. Somehow, I just know. I noticed him doing it earlier when he was reading, but to claim that would only make it seem like I've been watching him. Besides, it could be anyone. It could be me if I didn't know it wasn't.

"Anyone want to admit they do the same?"

"I mean, doesn't everyone?" Mara asks with a shrug.

"I don't," Austin says, "not really. I guess I don't really connect with the characters like that."

"So, if a book says a character wrinkles their nose, you don't do it, too?" Mara challenges.

"Nope," he says, popping the p. "Never."

She leans back in her seat, crossing her arms. "I'm going to watch you the next time you read."

"You like watching me," he teases, mouth hung open with a jeering expression. He pulls out the next slip of paper. "Okay, this one says, 'I've never read a classic.'"

"Well, we know that's not Memphis," Paulette chimes in, pointing a finger at him.

He lifts his head with a laugh. "Definitely not."

"I'll bet it's Paulette," Logan says.

"I haven't read a classic," she admits. "Unless *Twilight* counts? But that one's not mine. There's no shame in this girl's game. You know I'd tell you."

Austin pulls out the next one. "'I've never reread a book.'"

"That one's mine," Paulette says loudly, hopping up out of her chair.

"Never?" Memphis asks. "Not even one?"

"Not unless you count books from when I was a kid." She sits back down slowly, gulping more of her wine. "Who has time to reread books now?"

"But you get new stuff out of them every time," I tell her. "And you get to pick up on all of the little clues along the way. I love rereading."

"Eh." She shrugs. "It just sounds terrible. Like rewatching a movie you've already seen."

"You don't rewatch movies?" Logan leans forward so quickly he nearly falls out of his chair.

She shakes her head. "Ew, no. Never. Once I've seen it once, I get it."

"What about Christmas movies? My sister and I rewatch *Home Alone* every year," Mara says.

"Guys, I don't rewatch things. Period." She laughs. "I'm weird, I know. It's just not my thing."

Austin pulls the next one from the bowl, reading it silently. Suddenly, his face goes still. His Adam's apple bobs as he swallows and looks up, trying and failing to smile.

"What is it?"

"I, um, well...this one says, 'Sometimes I feel like because I've read so many dark stories about terrible things that I could get away with murder.'" He pauses, still staring at the paper. "'And sometimes, I kind of want to try.'"

A block of ice slides down my spine as chills spiderweb

across my arms. Next to me, Mara's hand slides across the couch to grip my wrist.

"What the hell?" Memphis asks, leaning forward over his knees.

Austin holds it out, showing us what's written. "Who wrote this?"

Our eyes search each other's, but to no one's surprise, the confession isn't claimed.

"It's not funny, guys," Mara says. "Don't joke about stuff like that." She's staring at Memphis, but he doesn't seem to have noticed.

"Seriously, not cool," Paulette agrees.

"Someone's probably just making a joke," Logan says softly, still studying us.

"Well, it's a dumb one." Austin wads up the paper and gathers the rest, standing to take the bowl into the kitchen.

"Where are you going?" Paulette asks, joining him on her feet.

"Game's over," he says. "Apparently someone has had a little bit too much to drink."

With that, Memphis grabs his coffee and heads from the room, and I drain the wine in my glass, disappearing in the opposite direction.

No one tries to stop either of us.

CHAPTER EIGHT

After the game, my social battery is drained. I'm exhausted, confused about what happened, and need a moment alone. I consider going to my room, but somehow that feels colder than I want it to. It was just a stupid game, and someone was obviously trying to shake us all up. I won't let it get to me. I don't want them to think anything is wrong or that I'm really mad or upset over what happened. So, instead, while everyone is trying to figure out what to do next and recovering from the chilling confession, I sneak back outside to the porch to read.

Of course, this also gives me the perfect opportunity to keep an eye on the house next door, but that's mostly coincidental.

The night air is cool and crisp, and a hint of smoke from somewhere in the distance bites at my nose. When the wind blows, I hear the soft hum of the breeze through the leaves, and I get the sense a storm might be on its way.

Try as I might, I can't stop myself from looking over at

the house next door. It's dark there. I don't see a single light on, but their black sedan is in the driveway. Could they have already gone to bed?

It's just after eight, so it's not impossible, but it seems strange. I can't explain why I'm so invested in this couple except to say that while my ex never laid a finger on me in that way, I know the look in her eyes well. The fear was palpable. She was clearly afraid of him, or uncomfortable at the very least, and I can't help feeling solidarity with her.

As if I'm her only hope.

I just wish I could catch her outside alone to let her know I'm here and will help if there's any way I can.

I pull out my tablet and open the book I've been reading, folding my legs up in the rocking chair to get comfortable.

I rock back and forth slowly with the chair, its wooden legs groaning against the floor of the porch.

Creeeeeaak.

Creeeeeaak.

Creeeeeaak.

Creeeeeaak.

Creeeeeaak.

I don't know how long I've been reading when I hear the noise that interrupts the silence. The soft *crunch, crunch* of leaves underfoot.

Someone is outside.

The realization sends a jolt of fear shooting through me. Someone is outside with me. In the dark. If it's the neighbor, if he's coming to get me, I'm not sure I'll be able to get inside in time or whether getting inside would do any good anyway.

Crunch, crunch.

Shhhhhhhhhh.

Crunch, crunch.

I listen carefully, trying to decide where the noise is coming from. It's pitch-black out here, only the glow of my tablet allows me to see anything.

I lock the screen, not wanting to give anyone a hint as to where I am and sit in silence.

Several seconds pass before a new scent fills my nose. Skunky. It's a scent I haven't smelled in years but one I recognize instantly.

Weed.

Someone is smoking weed nearby. I sit still, trying to decide what to do. It could just as easily be one of my housemates—Paulette and Austin immediately come to mind—as the neighbor, but I'm not sure if they know I'm out here, and since I don't really want company, I don't want to make my presence known if they haven't realized where I am.

I draw my legs up closer to me and remain still.

Then I hear it again.

Crunch, crunch.

Shhhhhhhhhh.

Crunch, crunch.

My heart thuds in my chest, sweat gathering at my brow. Why did I have to stick my nose where it didn't belong? Why did I come outside earlier when I heard a noise? And why did I come outside this late at night alone, for that matter? I should've just gone to my room, I know I should've, but somehow that felt more—

"Who's there?" A familiar voice fills the air as the

glowing butt of his joint appears from around the corner of the house.

"Austin? Is that you?" Relief floods me. *Thank God. Oh, thank God.*

He chuckles, the orange glow moving closer to me as I hear him climbing up the stairs.

"What are you doing out here, Lena Bena? Lena-Lin? Little Lena? Itty bitty Lena-tina?" He seems to be cracking himself up.

"I was reading." I unlock my tablet once more. "You scared the crap out of me."

"Sorry," he says. "Didn't mean to. Mind if I join you?" I don't get a chance to answer before he sits down in the chair next to me. "Want a hit?" He passes it toward me, but I shake my head in the glow of my tablet.

"No thanks."

"More for me." He pulls it back to his lips. "So, that was weird earlier, hm?"

"Yeah." My voice is soft in the silent night, so low I wonder if he heard me.

"Hey, can I ask you somethin'?" He turns his head toward me, blowing out a puff of smoke.

"Uh, sure."

"What's up with you and Ethan?"

I'm grateful he can't see the way my cheeks flush with heat in the darkness.

"What do you mean?"

He flicks his joint a few times, resting his hand on his knee. "I mean, are you a thing?"

"Um, no." The sound that releases from my lips is

somewhere between a laugh and a snort. "How could we be? We've never even met."

"I know. I just...well, I heard you talking to the girls when we all got here, and you seemed really upset when you found out he wasn't coming."

"Oh. Well, yeah, but just because we're friends. I was sad he was going to miss this when he put so much work into planning it."

"And you're sure that's it?" he presses.

"Yeah, of course. Why?"

"Okay, cool, because...I don't know. I think it'd be pretty cool if you and me, like, I don't know. I think you're really, um, hot." He chuckles under his breath, clearly feeling his high. "And I don't know if you think I am, too, but...you know, I don't want to overstep on Ethan's girl, but if you two aren't a thing, maybe *we* could be?"

"A thing?"

"I mean...I don't know. You feeling this, too, or am I dreaming?"

I put my head down, guilt weighing on me. "I'm— Austin, I'm coming off a really bad divorce. The last thing I need right now is a relationship." Memphis's face flashes in my mind. I'd be lying to myself if I said I don't feel something for him, even if I'm not sure what that is.

"I know about the divorce. I mean, I remember when you posted about it last year, and I was really sorry to hear it. I don't know if you saw it, I mean, you had a ton of comments obviously, but I commented to tell you how sorry I was. And, you know, this thing between you and me, it doesn't have to be anything serious. Or maybe it can be, eventually. But I'm cool with taking it a day at a time. Or...a weekend at a time, you know? As in, this weekend. If you're into it?"

I swallow, thinking not only about Memphis but also about the way I've seen Mara looking at Austin since we arrived. She hasn't outright said she wants to date him or anything like that, other than to say he's attractive, and she might want to hook up, but I know she's interested in him in one way or another. And I'm just...not.

"I'm not sure," I say eventually. "I'm sorry. I really value your friendship, but I'm just not ready for anything like that right now."

He stands abruptly. "Hey, no worries, man. No worries at all. I'm just here, you know? We're all here. Figured I might as well shoot my shot. You do you, girl." He laughs under his breath again, taking a last hit of the joint before he stubs it out on the railing and tosses it onto the ground. "I'll see you inside, yeah?"

"Yep. Yeah. See you in there."

With that, he opens the back door and enters the house again. I huff a breath, so shocked by what just happened. I've gotten the vibe Austin may be interested in me, but he's also been flirty with Mara and Paulette, so I was beginning to think that was just his personality.

I'm not sure if I should mention this to Mara or if it would only hurt her. I don't think she's in love with him or anything, but if the reverse happened with Ethan or Memphis—if either of them had hit on Paulette or Mara—it would've stung.

"Stop!"

A scream tears through the night, interrupting my racing, chaotic thoughts. I freeze in place, every hair on my arms standing on end.

What the—

"Ahhhhhhhhh!"

There's another scream from the neighbor's house as a light comes on in their kitchen. I look over, and with their blinds open, I am staring directly into the brightly lit room.

No.

No.

I try to make sense of what I'm seeing, but nothing about this scene makes sense. The woman is there, standing in the center of the room, looking at someone I can't see with horror in her expression. Dark crimson stains cover her beige shirt, her hands, her arms.

Blood.

There's blood in her hair, dripping down the side of her face.

There's nothing else it could be.

He's stabbed her. Shot her, maybe.

She's dying.

She looks out into the night, and though I know it's impossible, it's as if she's looking right at me in the dark of the night. She collapses on the ground, and adrenaline surges through me. I'm standing before I realize I've moved, panic-filled thoughts racing and rebounding through my mind. I rush to the railing, gripping on to it with all my might as if it's an invisible force keeping me from going any farther.

But I should.

I should do something.

I should go over there.

I should call the police.

I should scream.

I should get someone.

My phone is inside.

My phone is inside.

My phone is inside.

If I go over there, I'll die.

The light flicks off, bathing the house in darkness, and I shake my head free of the wild and chaotic thoughts. I turn and grab for the door, pulling it open and darting inside, nearly colliding with Logan, who was walking into the living room with a full glass of some dark liquid I suspect is red wine.

"Whoa, slow down. Where's the fire?" he asks, lifting his glass to keep from spilling it.

I zip past him, up the stairs, and toward my room.

"Lena!" I hear him shouting. "Are you okay?"

"No," I cry, searching for my phone. I find it where I left it on the nightstand and lift it with shaking hands. Of course, my FaceID doesn't work in the dim light, and I can't seem to get my fingers to cooperate.

"What's wrong?" That's Mara.

I turn to find everyone in my doorway staring at me with terrified expressions.

"I, um, I..." Finally my phone unlocks, and I dial the numbers—911. "*Lock the doors! Now!*" I order them.

"What?" Austin asks.

"Why?" Memphis asks, walking toward me.

Mara approaches me, too, with her hand held out. "What's going on, babe? What happened?"

"9-1-1, what's your emergency?" a woman's voice asks in my ear.

Every jaw in the room goes slack as the next words leave my mouth. "I need help. My neighbor just killed his wife."

CHAPTER NINE

Despite the urgency of the situation, it takes just under an hour for the police and ambulance to arrive on our street.

"Just three cop cars?" Logan asks.

"Maybe that's all they have," says Mara. "Small town."

"It's a murder," Austin points out. "They should be calling in the state police. The FBI. Something." He pauses, his eyes widening. "Do you think they're going to want to talk to us?"

"I don't think they call in the FBI for murder," Memphis says skeptically. "And yeah, probably. You might want to go...freshen up."

Nodding, Austin darts upstairs. With him gone, we watch from the side window in the foyer as the officers step from their cars and approach the dark house. They knock several times, and then, when there's no answer, they kick in the front door all too easily.

Then, the officers disappear inside.

It's another half an hour before they arrive on our front step. To my dismay and utter confusion, I don't see them leading the man out in handcuffs or a stretcher being wheeled out to the ambulance.

When a knock sounds on the door, we exchange worried glances, doing the customary thing you do when a food delivery arrives and waiting several seconds to pretend as if you aren't standing just inside the door awaiting their arrival.

It's Memphis who pulls open the door. Austin stays near the back of the group. "Officers."

Two officers stand in front of us: a tall, thin man with a bald head and a shorter man with brown, buzz-cut hair and a smattering of freckles across his nose and cheeks. It's the one with freckles who speaks first. "I'm looking for Lena Ortega."

"That's me." My sea of friends parts, allowing me to step forward.

"You placed the 9-1-1 call regarding a situation at your neighbor's house?"

I nod.

"Okay. I'm Officer Washington. This is Officer Montgomery. May we come inside?"

We step back and allow the officers into the foyer. Once inside, they both scan the room, and Officer Montgomery lets out a whistle. "This is a nice place you have here."

"We're just renting it for the weekend," Mara volunteers. "We aren't from here."

"I see. What brought you to town?" Officer Washington asks.

"Our friend, Ethan, rented the place as a little getaway," I tell them.

"Which one of you is Ethan?" he asks, pointing to the

three men, then, somewhat hesitantly, toward the rest of us.

"He's not here. He had something come up at the last minute."

"Okay." He clicks his tongue and looks at his partner. "So, Ms. Ortega, can you describe to me in detail what you saw tonight through your neighbor's window?"

I replay the events of the night for him—the scream and seeing the woman covered in blood.

"And did anyone else see this? Anyone else that can corroborate your story?" I don't like the way he asks this, and I know without him saying it that he doubts my story. Perhaps he suspects me of killing her. He looks up at the rest of the group again. Everyone around me shakes their heads slowly. "Alright, kids, how much have you all had to drink tonight?"

"A few drinks," I answer defensively.

"Lena has had less than anyone," Memphis says, stepping closer to me. "She's not drunk. She knows what she saw."

"Well, maybe so, but we just checked out the entire house next door, and there is no sign of struggle. Definitely no sign of a murder. No blood, nothing is broken or damaged. It's spotless."

"What?" My blood runs cold. "That's impossible. No. I know what I saw. He killed her. She was on the ground, drenched in blood. She was dying!"

"Maybe there was a glare on the window," the officer offers, his tone snarky and demeaning. "Maybe it was a trick of the light. Maybe you had too much to drink. Low blood sugar. I'm not totally sure, but I can promise you, Ms. Ortega, whatever you think you saw, you were mistaken."

He sighs and claps his hands together. "We're working on contacting the owners right now to explain the door we had to break into, but we're having no luck. I don't suppose you have a way to get in touch with them?"

"What? No," I say. "Why would we?"

"Have you had any contact with them since you arrived?" Officer Montgomery asks.

"No. We've seen them in passing a few times," I say. "I have, I mean. And Memphis." I point to him.

"We saw them earlier today, yeah," he confirms. "But only briefly, like she said."

"Mmkay, well"—he pulls a business card from his breast pocket and hands it to Memphis—"if you guys think of anything, give us a call, okay? We're going to have officers posted up outside to keep an eye out for anything suspicious until we can get ahold of the owners, but we shouldn't need anything else from you all right now. When do you leave town?"

"Sunday," I say.

"Okay. Be sure to stick around until then in case we have more questions. For now, just...lock your doors and stay inside for the night."

His words run through me. If they don't believe me, why are they telling us to stay inside? Why are they acting like we might be in danger?

"Do you think he's still around here?" I ask.

"I don't know what to think, ma'am," he says, taking a step toward the door. "But I'll tell you this, we're going to find out the truth about tonight."

Somehow, his words feel more like a warning than a reassurance.

CHAPTER TEN

No one can sleep.

I guess there's no surprise there. I half expected everyone to agree with the police, that I'd somehow imagined what I saw. That I was wrong or drunk or...God, high somehow from the second-hand smoke off of Austin's joint.

I know it's ridiculous, but I can't say each of those thoughts hasn't run through my head as well. No matter what anyone says, I know what I saw. I *know* it.

I just have to figure out how to prove it.

The man must've taken her body somewhere. But where? I don't know anything about them, but the woods seem like the most obvious place. Could he be hiding out there right now?

I glance toward the window as the rain sets in, a bolt of lightning illuminating the sky and giving the room an even more sinister vibe.

We're all in the living room—the girls on the couch on either side of me, and Austin, Memphis, and Logan in the armchairs. We each have our books, but no one is even pretending to read.

It's too terrifying.

The police have all left, aside from a single squad car that was parked along the side of the road last time we checked, which, if I had to guess, was about seven minutes ago.

I suppose it should make me feel safer that the police are hanging around in case the man returns, but I can't forget the way the officers looked at me. I know they suspect I'm wrong, at best, or lying about something, at worst.

I'm worried I'm going to have made the man mad. That he's going to try to hurt me when the police tell him I called them. Will they give him my name? Will he come after me? How far will he go to keep me quiet when I've already told the police everything?

And, more than anything else, I'm worried about the woman. I can't get the look in her eyes when she fell to the floor, the blood coating her shirt and skin, out of my mind. These aren't the sort of things you sleep after.

When my phone begins to ring from where it rests on the coffee table in front of me, everyone in the room turns to look at it. I lean down to see the caller ID, which reads **Davis County Sheriff's Office.**

I lift my phone, preparing myself for the worst—that they've found the body or that they're going to arrest me for filing a supposedly fake police report—and swipe my thumb across the screen. "Hello?"

"Lena Ortega?" I recognize Officer Montgomery's voice at once.

"Yes."

"This is Officer Montgomery. We spoke earlier."

"Yes, I remember." My body is ice cold.

"I'm calling to let you know we were able to reach the owners of the house next door."

"You were?" He said *owners.* Plural. I didn't miss that.

"I'm happy to report they are both alive and well. They're out of town and have been for quite some time."

"That's impossible," I say softly, half convinced I've fallen asleep and this is a dream. A nightmare I can't wake up from. "Did you speak to both of them? He could've been lying—"

"I spoke to Mrs. Hawthorne first, then her husband, yes. They assured me that they are fine and out of town. They also confirmed there's been no one staying at their house. So, no one is quite sure what you think you saw, but I want to reassure you that it was nothing. Everything is fine."

I shake my head. "It's...no. I know what I saw. I couldn't have imagined all of this. Seeing them two different times. And seeing...what I saw tonight. No. There were people staying in that house. A couple. A man and a woman. We saw them twice before tonight."

Around me, everyone is leaning closer, trying to understand what I'm being told.

"I'm sorry, Ms. Ortega. We have no reason to believe there was anyone in that house tonight, or this weekend for that matter. Now, I want to believe you know better than to try and pull this off as some sort of prank, and I hope I'm not wrong about that. The owners will be returning soon, and we've asked our officers to go back to the house at that point to talk with them. For tonight, we're going to end our surveillance of the house. We have no reason to believe you'll be unsafe, but you can feel free to call me back at this number if you have any issues, okay?"

I swallow and barely manage to squeak, "Okay."

He has just accused me of lying to the police. Of reporting a crime that didn't happen. Of doing all of this as some sort of...prank. Why would I do that? That's illegal, isn't it? Am I going to get in some sort of trouble?

I feel as if I'm going to be sick.

I don't know how the call ends, but eventually it does, and everyone is waiting for me to tell them all I've learned. But I can't. I can't say anything at all because one single, terrifying truth is repeating over and over in my head.

The officers outside—our only source of protection and safety—are leaving, and soon, the man will be back.

CHAPTER ELEVEN

The police waste no time leaving. In fact, by the time we make it to the window to check, all we can see of them are taillights.

"I don't get it. How can they just leave?" Logan asks.

"Because they don't believe us," I say, my voice powerless and defeated.

"We need to go," Paulette says, running a hand through her hair. "We need to get out of here before these psychos get back."

"If we leave, we look guilty," I point out.

"Better than looking dead," she argues, on the brink of losing it.

"Lena's right," Memphis says. "We can't leave. They told us to stay put until Sunday. We'll lock the doors. I can stay awake and keep an eye on things. If they come back, we'll call the police again."

"Because they were such a help last time," Paulette scoffs.

"I'm not stopping anyone who wants to leave,"

Memphis says, "but I'm staying. And it sounds like Lena is staying."

"I'll stay, too," Mara says, taking my hand in hers. I look over, and she gives me a reassuring nod and bumps my arm playfully. "I told you I got you."

"Me, too," Austin says. "I'm not leaving Lena here alone. Or anyone, for that matter. We're safer together."

Logan and Paulette look at each other, and Paulette groans. Logan raises one shoulder with a shrug.

"What do you think?" he asks.

"Fine," she says with an attitude, "but I'm not sleeping alone."

She barely gets the sentence out before Logan volunteers as tribute. "I'll stay with you."

"I can stay with you if you want, Lena," Austin offers. My stomach drops.

Memphis opens his mouth with what I expect is an objection, but Mara speaks up first. "I've got her. We'll bunk together."

"Oh, okay. Cool." Austin steps back.

"Not that any of us will be sleeping," I add dryly.

"Come on. Let's try not to think about it anymore, right guys?" Mara looks around the room, trying to garner encouragement, but she receives none. "I'm sure it's nothing," she says finally. "You know, I bet it's probably just...a Halloween prank or something."

"A month late?" Austin asks.

"You guys believe me, don't you?" I ask them, almost too scared to know their answers.

"Of course we believe you," Mara says quickly. "A thousand percent. If you say you saw it, you saw it. And anyone who says otherwise has to fight me." She wrinkles her nose at me, trying to force the joke, but I can't summon the strength to smile.

"I mean, Memphis saw the neighbors, too. I didn't make them up." I point at him, and he nods, shoving a hand in his pocket.

"I mean, yeah, I saw a couple outside today. But... maybe they were the cleaners or something, if the owners really are out of town."

"Maybe," I agree. We never actually spoke with them to know the truth. Maybe we'll never know who they were. Maybe the woman will just disappear, like so many others. "Maybe we should go over there and check it out." My voice shakes as I make the suggestion—one my entire body is revolting against.

Mara's grip tightens on my hand. "No. Lena, it's not safe. We can't."

"She's right," Memphis says. "No way are we going over there. Whatever's going on, let the police handle it."

"No way in hell," Austin agrees. "We're locking this place up like Fort Knox, and no one so much as cracks a curtain until morning."

"Fine," I say, not sure whether to feel frustrated or relieved.

With that settled and with nothing left to say, we all retreat to our rooms. Mara wraps her arm around my shoulders on the way up the stairs, and we get ready for bed quietly. Neither of us seems to know quite what to say.

When we get into bed, Mara loops her arm through mine, a promise without words to stick together no matter what.

"Thank you for believing me," I whisper, tears burning the back of my throat.

"Always," she promises. "I told you we'd get through this weekend together, and I meant it. It's going to be okay. You'll see. Tomorrow, once the sun is up, everything will seem a lot less scary."

I force a smile she can't see.

In the silence, she stifles a yawn, then adds, "I really wish they had TVs in the bedrooms so we could watch *Friends* or something. Chandler always makes me feel better after I've watched a scary movie."

"Could this trip *be* any worse?" I ask, trying to make her laugh even when I can't.

She snuggles up against me. All too soon, I feel her breathing growing slower and then, a soft, breathy snore comes from the back of her throat. I'm glad she can sleep, really I am, but I can't help feeling bitter about my inability to drift off with such ease.

The room feels smaller tonight. Stuffier.

Soon, the entire right side of my body is coated with sweat from where our bodies are touching. I've never liked sleeping so close to anyone. Never liked sharing space like this.

Maybe that's why my marriage didn't work.

I swallow, carefully easing my arm out of the tangle of hers and trying not to wake her. I stick one leg out of the covers in an attempt to cool down.

My throat is too dry. I reach down and scratch my leg, scraping sweat from my skin. I roll to my side, then back, shove a hand under my pillow, then pull it back out.

For what must be the next several hours, I toss and

turn, trying and failing to find a comfortable position, covering and uncovering to find a temperature that fits.

When I can't, when nothing seems to be working, I give up. With a huff, I toss the covers off of me and slip out of the bed. If I keep this up, I'm going to wake Mara, and that's the last thing she needs. She deserves her sleep, even if I can't get any.

I tiptoe across the room and ease the door open. Staring out into the dark hallway, I instantly regret my decision. *What am I thinking?*

After everything that happened, the last thing I need right now is to be alone in a dark house. I glance back at the bed, where Mara is sleeping peacefully, and steel myself. I grip the door handle.

I'm going to be fine.

There is no one in this house but us.

I'm safe.

I pull the door closed and step into the hall. The cool air hits me on the staircase, fresh and chilly from the open space downstairs. On the first step, the staircase groans, and I wince, hoping I haven't woken anyone else up.

I listen carefully, certain I hear Paulette moving around in her bedroom, but I don't stop to investigate.

Instead, I take the next step, moving down the staircase and to the bottom floor. I'll just get a glass of ice water and then head back upstairs.

Just something to calm my nerves.

I walk down the hall and toward the kitchen, and when I arrive, my heart stops. Standing in the dark, next to the island, I can just barely make out the silhouette of a person.

I take half a step back as my brain struggles to process what I'm seeing.

Then—

"Can't sleep either?"

"Oh my god! Memphis!" The words come out on a breath. A gasp. A sigh of relief. "I thought you were..." I don't know how to finish the sentence. I have no idea who I thought he was. The man from next door, most likely, but I'm not sure what to call him or how that would make any sense. "You scared the crap out of me. What are you doing down here?"

"Same thing as you, I'd guess. I couldn't sleep," he says simply.

I sigh. My hands are still shaking as I cross the room and pull open a cabinet, feeling for a glass in the dark. The only light in the house right now is the moonlight coming through the windows.

I move toward the fridge and fill my glass with cool water from the dispenser.

When I'm done, I look down, not turning back to face him. "I know what I saw," I whisper.

He's quiet for a long time.

When I spin back around, I repeat myself, this time louder. "I know what I saw, Memphis."

"I heard you."

"Why didn't you answer?"

"Because I don't want to talk about it."

I step toward the island, placing my glass down. "Well, I do."

"Well, go talk to Mara, then."

"She's asleep. I'm talking to you." I have no time for his games or his grumpy mood right now.

"Look, I have no idea what's going on and, frankly, that terrifies me. But there's nothing we can do by freaking ourselves out talking about it."

"You saw the couple," I remind him.

"I know I did."

"But you don't believe me?"

He steps toward me, seemingly without realizing he's done it. "I never said that."

"You didn't have to."

"Lena, I believe you. It's just...I wish you were wrong."

I drop my chin to my chest, running a finger along the rim of my glass. "I wish I was, too."

"I don't understand what's going on or why the police didn't find anything at the house. All I want to do is keep you safe and get you out of here, but leaving feels worse somehow, and I—" He cuts himself off. "I just fucking hate this."

It's my turn to step toward him, and I come to stop just a few inches in front of his chest. I rest my hand on the island, sliding it across the granite top until I feel his fingers. I stop there, my heart racing, throat tight. "Thank you for wanting to keep me safe."

He's as still as a statue. "Don't read too much into it."

"I would never," I whisper.

I hear, rather than see, him swallow. "Good."

"Good."

He pulls his hand back, and I miss it immediately. Before I can withdraw mine, I feel him turn his over, sliding it back under mine so our fingers can lace together loosely.

He's not holding my hand, but the feeling is just as nice. It makes me feel just as safe.

"I hated when Austin said he was going to stay in your room," he whispers, his voice throaty.

"Why?"

He inhales sharply, but no answer comes. I can feel the weight of his stare in the darkness, practically hear the internal war he has going on.

"I wasn't going to let him," I say finally.

"He likes you, you know."

"He likes everyone," I say flatly. "And, for the record, he already tried to shoot his shot with me tonight, and I said no."

I feel him tense. "Oh."

"After the game," I add. "He came outside to talk to me and said we should hook up." I don't know why I'm telling him this, only that I have the desperate need to fill the silence somehow. "I said I'm not interested." I start to mention that Mara likes him but barely find the will to stop myself in time.

He scoffs. "We finished the game on that little high note, and he still thought it was the perfect time to hit on you."

"Well, to his credit, I think he's been trying all weekend. On all of us, really. I just happened to be the one who was most available this evening, apparently. Besides, Austin isn't..."

He moves half an inch closer to me, and I feel the warmth of his skin in the space between us. "Isn't what?"

I had started to say Austin wasn't the type to read a

room but changed my thought midway through. "Isn't my type," I say instead.

"Your type?"

"Mm-hmm."

"And what is your type?" His fingers swipe over mine slowly, rhythmically.

A wave of heat passes over me, and I realize he's moved even closer. His knee bumps against mine gently, and I see his hand move toward my waist, though he doesn't actually touch me. It's as if we're being drawn together like magnets, neither of us capable of stopping it.

My ears burn as I stare up at him in the darkness, his features hardly readable, all shadows and sharp angles.

"Rich, clearly," I say finally, forcing a joke that makes him laugh and breaks the tension at once. "And, remind me, yours is...wildly attractive and unemployed?"

He steps back with a laugh, the spell broken, and I miss him so much I hate it.

"Don't forget an insomniac. Someone to keep me company at night." He takes another step back and takes a sip of his coffee.

"While you reread boring books and make the faces the characters do? You know, if you stopped drinking coffee so much, you might actually be able to sleep."

"Where's the fun in that?" he teases. "This is when I get all my reading done."

"Well, I'm sorry I interrupted."

"I'm not." His voice comes out strangled, as if he hadn't meant to say it, and tried to stop it halfway through.

"Good to know," I say softly, taking another sip of my drink. I tap my fingers on the granite top of the island.

"Who do you think wrote that creepy message in the game earlier?"

"Truth be told, I assumed it was Paulette."

"Paulette?" My brows draw together. "Why?"

"I don't know. It just seemed like the kind of thing she'd do for a laugh, but she claimed one of the others was hers, so who knows?"

"We should've just stuck with Truth or Dare or something." I groan, running a hand through my hair and stifling a yawn.

"Are you tired?"

I shake my head. "Not too tired, no."

"Truth?" he presses, stepping toward me again.

"What if I wanted a dare?" I tease, poking his stomach.

He grabs my hand, holding it still, and I swallow. His warmth is so overwhelming and comforting it makes my whole body tingle.

"I'm tired," I admit, "but I'm scared if I go to sleep, I'll see it—see her—again."

He slides his hand up my arm slowly, releasing a slow breath through his nose. Then, both arms come around me, and he pulls me into a hug. His chin rests atop my head as he holds me, saying nothing at all.

Somehow, it's exactly what I needed.

Cool tears collect in my eyes, and I fight against them with everything in me. If I cry, my tears will soak through his shirt, and he'll know. I can't let him see how fragile I am. I won't survive it.

"Your turn," I whisper, pulling back and pretending to scratch my cheeks as I brush my tears away. If he realizes that's what I'm doing, he's kind enough not to mention it.

"My turn?"

"Truth or dare?"

"We're not actually playing that game."

"Oh, no. You don't get to back out now. Truth or dare, Memphis?"

"Truth," he says finally.

I think for a moment. I'd been counting on him choosing a dare instead. Finally, I turn to lean back against the island and stare at him standing next to me. "What happened with the other person you were attracted to?"

It takes him a long time to answer. "Other person?"

"You said you don't hire people you're attracted to because it hasn't worked out for you in the past. Why? What happened?"

"Oh." He turns, resting his back against the island, too, so we're shoulder to shoulder. "There's no real story. My parents hired someone before Mary, and we had a short thing. It ended awkwardly for everyone, and she left. Lesson learned."

"I'm sorry." I nudge his arm with mine.

"Don't be. It wasn't serious. I just...learned to never mix business with pleasure."

The word *pleasure* on his lips sends a zing of electricity through my body. I study him, trying to read his expression in the dark room. He opens his mouth, and I wait for what he's going to say next. I shouldn't be feeling this way about him, whatever way that is. It doesn't make sense to me. And yet, it's the only thing that does make sense.

"Your turn," he whispers, turning slightly so he's facing me.

"Truth."

"Why are you still down here?"

I swallow. "What? Because I'm talking to you, obviously."

"That's the only reason?"

Every atom in my body is alive with electricity and adrenaline, my skin buzzing as we move closer together. "What other reason would there be?"

"You tell me." He raises his hand as he moves to stand in front of me, bringing it to rest on my hip.

"I was thirsty."

He laughs, his breath hitting my skin. We're just inches apart, his warm, earthy scent filling my nose. He clicks his tongue. "I don't think you're telling the truth."

"I like talking to you," I admit. "And I don't know why."

"Tell me about it," he whispers, and finally, we're in complete agreement about something. We don't make any sense together, and yet I find myself drawn to him in a way I've never been drawn to anyone. Just a day ago, I hated him and wished I hadn't come on this trip because he was here. Now, that feels preposterous. He lifts a hand, again not really seeming like he knows he's doing it, and cups my jaw, his thumb resting on my cheek. "It's driving me crazy."

"What is?" I whisper, resting my forehead against his before I realize I've moved.

"You are. This is. Whatever this is."

I'm not sure there's a word for it or that putting a word to it won't somehow ruin this. I'm not sure we're not both just running on pure adrenaline from the events of the evening, or that exhaustion isn't getting the better of us.

What I know is that when his eyes close, so do mine.

And when I feel his chin tilting toward mine, I meet him inch for inch. I shouldn't want this, but I do.

Something is very, very wrong with me.

"Lena, I—"

THUMP.

We wrench apart at the sound of a soft noise across the room. I turn, trying to make out where the sound came from or what it was. Memphis moves away from me, heading for the sound, and flips on a light as he goes.

"Did you hear that?" he asks from the doorway.

"It sounded like someone bumped into something. A table, maybe. Or a chair." I follow quickly behind him, not wanting to be left alone.

"Who's there?" he calls, shouting into the dining room before he flips on the light in there. The room is empty and nearly silent; the only sound is that of the soft *tick* of the clock above the fireplace.

He circles the table, then leads me out into the living room to check there. The stack of books we used earlier to place our papers on during the game is scattered across the floor, but other than that, nothing seems out of place.

"Was this like that before?" He gestures toward the stack.

"I...I think so." I try to remember. "I don't know if anyone stacked them up after the game."

"Logan would've, though. Right?" He checks over his shoulder, looking out the window.

"Maybe not. We were all frazzled after that weird confession."

He doesn't look convinced, but eventually, the worry fades from his face, replaced by a new expression that can only be described as regret. The weight of what happened between us in the dark kitchen now feels heavy in the lighted room.

He runs a hand through his hair. "It's an old house. Probably just the pipes or something."

I nod. "Right."

He clears his throat, looking down. "You should, uh, we should go to bed. *Separately*. I should go back to my room."

"Right. Yeah." I step backward. He's right, and still, it hurts. It feels like rejection.

"I, uh—"

"It's okay." I spin around, heading for the kitchen. "I'm tired, anyway. We'll talk tomorrow, yeah?"

Before he can answer, I disappear into the kitchen, then into the foyer, and back up the stairs. Every few seconds, I check over my shoulder, though I'm not sure if I'm looking for the source of the sound or for Memphis to follow me.

In the end, I find neither.

CHAPTER TWELVE

As soon as there's daylight outside, I slip out of bed and make my way out of the bedroom, not bothering to do anything more than brush my teeth.

To my utter mortification, I find Memphis sitting on the floor in the hallway, his back resting against the wall. He looks up at the sound of the door opening, rubbing his eyes with the back of his hand.

I shut the door softly, awkward energy coursing through me as I struggle to keep my voice low. "Hi."

He stands to his feet, his expression pained. "Hey."

"What are you doing out here? Why are you in the hall-way? Did something happen?" I think back to the night before, to the sound we heard. He'd have come to find me if he discovered the source, wouldn't he? If it was something more than the pipes in an old house?

"What? No. I was..." He stops, rethinking. "I was...just making sure nothing happened to you." Quickly, he adds, "*Any* of you."

"What? Why would you do that? The floor couldn't have been comfortable. You said you were going to bed."

"Well, I lied, I guess." When I open my mouth to scold him, he goes on, "Look, I told you I don't sleep well. I figured if I was in my room, it was a waste of my talent." His smile is more of a grimace than anything. "I'm fine, I swear. I'm just glad the sun's up. And, about last night—"

"We don't have to talk about it." I cut him off.

"I just wanted—"

"We were both tired. Delirious, even. We weren't thinking clearly, especially after the weird night. It's okay."

He swallows, the corners of his eyes wrinkling, and I know he wants to say more, but he doesn't press the issue any further. We make our way down the stairs and to the kitchen, where I see he has another pot of coffee already brewed. "It's still hot if you want some," he says, grabbing a mug from the kitchen island and filling it.

"You should really get some rest, Memphis. I'm awake now. I'll take over. This isn't healthy. You can't just *not* sleep."

"Eh, I dozed off a few times. Trust me, I'm good." He waves me off. "Well-rested. Couldn't sleep another wink."

"Well, are you rested enough to go next door with me?"

He groans. "Somehow I knew you were going to try that again."

"I have to know."

"Know what, Lena? The police already told you they didn't find anything there. What do you think you're possibly going to find that they missed? Literal professionals whose entire job it is to not miss anything."

"Well, one, that's not, like, their *entire* job. And two,

maybe they did overlook something. Everyone makes mistakes. "

He sips his coffee. "Like what? What are you counting on them having missed? A body?"

"Of course not." I try to think, not entirely sure what I'm hoping to find. "Blood, maybe. Or even a photo of them in a frame that proves they are actually real and live there. Something. Anything to prove what I saw last night actually happened."

He twists his lips. "I don't know. It's dangerous. I think they would've seen something if it was there to be found."

"They didn't want to believe me. You saw that. I doubt they even looked that hard once they realized they didn't see a body."

He sighs, setting his mug down. "Okay, fine. We'll walk outside and make sure the car isn't there, then we can see if the door is open. We'll take a quick look around and get back out of there. No hanging around, no snooping through boxes in the attic. In and out, that's it. Deal?"

"Fine." I turn toward the door but stop short. "And thank you."

"Yeah, yeah. No problem."

We slip on our shoes and make our way out the back door, stopping on the porch.

"I don't see their car. He's still gone," I whisper.

"Okay, let's go. Quickly." We cross the yard, looking entirely suspicious, I'm sure, if there is anyone around to see us.

When we reach the wraparound porch, I climb the stairs slowly with Memphis's hand against my back, his body heat hitting me from behind. It's so reminiscent of last night I have to squeeze my eyes shut to force away the memory.

The front door is cracked down the side and still standing partially open from the police's entry last night.

When I feel Memphis's hand drop away from my back, I look behind me to make sure he's still with me, and his face goes stoic as he gives me a little nod. With that assurance, we step inside.

I push the door open gently, allowing my eyes to adjust to the dark, silent room. We're in what looks like a mudroom, with shoes strewn about and jackets, coats, and scarves hanging up on a nearby coat rack.

I move forward carefully, minding my step as I have to climb two small stairs into the kitchen.

"This is where it happened," I whisper, pointing to the kitchen floor where I saw her fall. The hardwood floors are an ashy blonde color, and I bend down next to them, searching for any hint of blood in the cracks, but I find nothing.

I look up to find Memphis circling the island, eyes locked on the edge. "Just looking," he whispers when he notices me staring. "See anything?"

I shake my head. "Nothing." Standing up, I move to the living room and search for any photographs that would connect the couple to this house, but I find none. In fact, there are no personal photos in this room at all.

Only landscape photographs on canvases. There's very little here that I would consider personal. There are two doors on the wall in this room, and I push one open to find a small bathroom. I open the medicine cabinet, hoping to find a name, but there's only a small tube of antibiotic cream and a package of bandages, plus an expired bottle of allergy pills.

I leave the room and head for the next one, which is a bedroom, but again, there is nothing personal there. The home looks as if it belongs in a magazine. Small and quaint but pristine. As if no one lives here at all.

Maybe Memphis was right. Maybe those people were the cleaners. After all, we only saw them coming and going a few times, and the one time she was carrying a box. Perhaps it was a box of cleaning supplies.

I guess that would explain why he was able to clean up the murder scene so efficiently.

I cross the room and check out the window, running my finger along the ledge to check for dust. It wouldn't pass a white-glove test, but it's not overly dusty either. It's not completely impossible that the people were cleaners.

Turning around, I spot Memphis coming from another room off the kitchen. I raise my brows at him, but he shakes his head.

"Nothing. Just a bedroom, but it must be the guest room. There were just a few canvases on the wall, like in the living room."

"Same in the bedroom off the living room," I tell him. "I'm starting to think you were right about these people being cleaners. The house is spotless."

From where I'm standing, I can see the back porch of our house and the rocking chair where I was sitting last night.

I know what I saw. I know it.

I cross the room to stand where she was standing and try to remember exactly where in the room she was looking.

122

"She was staring in that direction," I whisper, looking toward the sink. "And there's the light switch. Maybe she turned it on and ran, but he caught her. The light wasn't on for long. Just a few seconds."

Maybe I was her only hope, and I failed her. Maybe, when she flipped the light on, all she could wish for was that I'd be sitting on the porch and see her in distress.

Maybe she wanted me to rush over, to try and stop him, but I didn't.

"It wasn't your fault," Memphis whispers, moving to stand in front of me. "You know that, right?"

I swallow, looking up at him. "I'm the only one who saw her. The only one who could've helped."

"No," he says, his tone angry. "You couldn't have. If he killed her, he would've killed you, too—"

"I could've tried—"

"You would've gotten yourself killed." He takes both sides of my face in his hands, staring down at me with such intensity I swear I feel the heat. His eyes flick down to my lips, then back up.

My heart thuds in my chest, thundering so loudly I can't hear my next breath. Down his eyes go again, landing and lingering on my lips.

"Lena, I..."

Just those simple words, the whisper of my name on his lips, sends a bolt of electricity through my body. He shouldn't be looking at me that way. I shouldn't be looking back.

I swallow. "Yeah?"

He draws his bottom lip into his mouth, running his tongue over it. "I—"

I freeze at the sound of a car approaching.

"Shit," he whispers. The car's tires slow down on the gravel and eventually come to a stop.

I shoot a glance at Memphis, whose dark eyes are now filled with only fear.

Outside, a car door shuts.

Someone's here.

CHAPTER THIRTEEN

Thinking quickly, Memphis grabs my arm and pulls me toward him and against the wall. I slam into him, keeping myself still as I try to listen to the sounds outside.

It's incredibly hard to do when I can focus on nothing except the way he's looking at me. Our chests rise and fall together, and I'm not sure whose heartbeat I'm feeling. His eyes lock with mine, and for a split second, that warm feeling fills my core again, something totally out of place in this moment of terror.

He looks away quickly, turning and lifting his head from the wall to take a peek out the window. I'm incredibly aware of his arm around my shoulders, his other hand resting gently on my hip.

His head falls back to the wall. "It's not them," he says softly, then juts his chin forward. "Go. Quick. Through the back. Come on."

He releases me too quickly, and I miss the heat of his skin against mine. *What the hell is wrong with me?*

I push away from him, tiptoeing across the kitchen, past the dining room table, and into the hallway. I pull open the first door we reach, staring down into darkness.

"A basement," Memphis whispers, peering inside.

"We should check it out—"

"We don't have time." He nudges me forward. "Keep going. Find the back door." Easing the door shut, we move forward quickly as I hear a muffled voice outside. I can't make out what they're saying, but I know they're close. Too close.

My heart races for a new reason now, as we have mere seconds to get out of this house before we're caught.

"There!" I whisper.

The back door is just in front of us, secured with a dead bolt and locked knob. I twist them both with shaking hands as I hear another door shut outside.

Faster.

Faster.

If we're caught in this house, there's no way we'll ever be able to explain why we're here.

I twist the knob and ease it open gently, stepping outside, and then we bolt. We run down the two concrete steps and across the lawn at full speed, only stopping when we've reached our own yard. I bend forward over my knees, huffing to catch my breath. Next to me, Memphis is panting, a small smile playing on his lips.

"We almost got caught," I say. "Why are you smiling?"

"I guess I'm an adrenaline junkie and never knew it."

"Well, then, you're welcome." I roll my eyes as I hear a voice and turn my head to look at them.

"Oh my god," a woman cries. Next to her, a man puts a hand on her shoulder. My entire body turns to ice as I stare at him, then slowly melts as I realize I'm wrong.

It's not him.

From a distance, he could pass for the man I saw before. He has similar curly, black hair, but this man's only goes to his chin, not down his back, and there's much more gray in his beard. He's also a bit heavier than the man who was here before, his features less sharp.

The woman covers her mouth with her hand as she stares in horror at the house, her red hair cascading down her back in a low ponytail.

As if they can sense us staring at them from where we stand next to our back porch, the man turns his head to look in our direction, searching for the source of whatever strangeness he's feeling. When his eyes land on us, the woman turns her head, too.

Unlike the first couple, these two walk toward us, moving down the porch and onto the grass with determination. In the driveway is a blue SUV that I haven't seen here before.

The man shields his eyes from the sun with his palm. "Hello there!" he calls warily.

My entire body is stiff as I feel Memphis step slightly in front of me. I move to stand next to him, refusing to be protected. Stubbornly, I find myself rebelling against the idea that I should be his to protect.

"Hi," I say.

"Can we help you?" Memphis asks.

"Are you the young woman who called the police last

127

night?" The man ignores Memphis and directs his attention at me.

"Yes, that was me."

He sighs, running a hand over his forehead. "Our front door has been destroyed because of this."

I jerk my head back. *That's* what they're worried about? Not about the poor woman who was murdered in their house?

"That door cost two thousand dollars," the woman says, her lips pinched together. "Do you really think the police are going to replace it?"

"A woman was hurt," I say angrily. "She needed help. What was I supposed to do?"

The man studies me, his thick eyebrows drawn down. "The police told us there was no sign of any break-in or any sort of altercation. No one was staying in our house."

"Could it have been your cleaners, perhaps?" I ask. "A man and a woman. She had shorter brown hair, and he had black curls like you."

The man and woman exchange an odd glance.

"Do you know who I'm talking about? They've been here twice since we arrived. And then last night, she was covered in blood in your kitchen. That's why I called the police."

She opens her mouth, but he's the one who speaks. "It's impossible. We don't have cleaners, no one broke in, and no one has a key to our house." He pauses, shaking his head. "Look, I don't know what you saw, but I'd appreciate you minding your business. There was no one in our house."

"Take it easy, man. She was just trying to help," Memphis says.

"Well, all her help did was force us to end our vacation early and figure out how to replace this door," the woman points out, massaging the space between her eyes. "Please, just...stay on your side of the yard." She waves a hand at me and turns, pulling her husband to walk away and lowering her voice as she says, "This was exactly what we were worried about when they started renting that house out to random strangers. What did I tell you?"

"Look, I know what I saw," I call after them. "Please. We aren't troublemakers, and we weren't trying to inconvenience you. There have been two people staying in your house all weekend. I swear I'm telling the truth. I've seen them a few different times. They drive a dark car and look about your age."

They stop briefly, and she turns to look over her shoulder at me. "We've told you, we have no idea what you're talking about. We don't know anyone who fits that description and, *again*, no one would've been able to get inside our house."

"Are you sure?" I push, stepping forward. "You didn't have a key hidden under a plant or a rug or something that someone could've found? Did you buy the house recently and forget to change the locks, maybe?"

They spin around to face us and she pins me with a glare. "Look, Nancy Drew, I think I would know if someone was allowed in my house. I don't need to answer to some child about any of this." She turns on her heels, pulling her husband to follow her. "Please don't try to help us anymore."

Memphis touches my arm. "Come on. Let's go back inside."

"They're wrong, Memphis. Or they're lying. They have to be."

He doesn't say anything, just nudges me forward gently while checking over his shoulder.

Bitter tears sting my eyes. "I know what I saw," I say. I'm not sure if I'm telling him or myself.

CHAPTER FOURTEEN

Back inside, everyone has finally woken up, though they're all blissfully unaware of the nightmare of a morning Memphis and I have experienced. When we make our way into the kitchen, Mara stands next to the toaster, humming a song as she waits for her breakfast.

"What's wrong?" Her face tells me what mine must look like.

"Um..." I don't even know where to begin. "Apparently, the real owners of the house next door just got home. Whoever was staying there before wasn't supposed to be there."

"What? Seriously?" she asks, shaking her head. "How did they get in?"

"I have no idea," I say.

Memphis moves past us and refills his coffee mug. "Doesn't matter. At this point, we all just need to move on. They said to leave them alone. They obviously don't want our help. So I say we just let it go."

I know he's really talking to me. Telling me to let it go.

I want to tell him I can't. To take back whatever moment we had in that house. I'm so angry with him for not...

Truth is, I don't know what I'm angry with him for or what else I expect him to do. I just know I'm angry.

"What's going on?" Austin asks, walking into the room with an empty plate that he places in the sink.

"The neighbors—the *actual* neighbors, apparently— just got here and told us to butt out of their business," Memphis says.

"Jesus," Austin mutters. "Really?"

"What jerks." Mara pulls me into her side. "I'm sorry, Lena. We all know you were just trying to help."

I shrug one shoulder. "It just doesn't make any sense. I saw her." Bitter tears prick my eyes once again, and I hate them and hate myself for them and hate this and hate everything. "I saw her with blood on her shirt. I saw her fall down. I know it... I know."

She rubs my back. "We believe you."

"But no one else does. The police don't. How are we going to help her if no one seems to know she exists?" I bury my face in my hands, so angry with myself for losing it right now. All I wanted to do was help.

"What do you want to eat?" Austin asks, opening a cabinet. "Everything's easier with a full stomach. Cereal? Toast? Oatmeal? Name it, and I'll make it." He looks guiltily at Mara. "And if it's too complicated, Mara will make it."

I laugh despite my tears. "I'm okay."

"You need to eat," Memphis says, his voice gruff. He

opens a cabinet and pulls out the bag of Starbursts. "Here. Breakfast of champions."

"I'll make you some toast," Mara says, eyeing the bag with disgust. "At least a few bites. You need something in your belly."

I don't argue, but I do pull out a Starburst and pop one in my mouth. Maybe it's a bad habit, but candy always makes me feel better. Besides, the thought of eating anything of actual substance when there are still so many unanswered questions makes me feel sick. Memphis hands me a mug of coffee without a word, and I take a sip of it, the warmth spreading throughout my body in an instant.

A few minutes later, Mara hands me a plate of toast, carefully smothered with butter and jam, and we join Logan and Paulette at the table.

Today, Paulette has a shirt on with a grinning opossum that says **I'm not like other girls. I'm worse.** and a pair of yoga pants with hot dogs on them. Logan sits next to her, holding her hand on the tabletop. They don't seem to notice we've entered the room until we sit down at the table.

Apparently, last night went really well for them.

Bitterness swells in my gut, and I'm disgusted with it.

Why should I not be happy for my friends?

Why don't they care that a woman is dead?

"I think we should focus on why we came," Mara says, keeping her voice gentle once we've sat down. "I know this weekend hasn't exactly gone as expected, but we came to read and hang out and relax. We still need to do some of the collaborations we've talked about, and we leave tomorrow morning, so we're running out of time." She looks at me, rubbing my arm. "But you tell us what you need, Lena. We're here for you. I'd just hate to see you leave this place regretting not getting to do whatever you wanted to. I'd hate to see these people ruin your vacation. I know how important it was to you."

She's right. This weekend was meant to be my first step back to independence. I'd saved up for it and pinned my hopes on what it would do to lift my spirits and get me back in a good place.

And now this.

"You're right," I say softly.

"Whatever's going on, you tried your best to help," Paulette adds. "You've done literally all you can do. No one can fault you for letting it go now." She reaches her hand across the table to take mine and squeezes it.

I take a bite of my toast, which is stupidly delicious for just being a piece of bread. "Thanks, guys. I'm sorry I've messed everything up this weekend."

"You didn't."

"What?"

"Don't say that."

"You didn't mess anything up."

"Lena..."

Everyone is quick to jump to my aid, to assure me I haven't messed anything up, which only makes me feel guiltier—as if this is all a pity party I've asked for.

I set the toast down and dust the crumbs from my fingers. "Okay, let's enjoy this last day, yeah? After breakfast, I say we get some pictures together, and then we can listen to some more of the audiobook Logan borrowed and make another dinner together."

Mara takes my hand. "The last dinner," she says somewhat nostalgically.

"At least this time," Austin agrees. "But we're totally doing this again."

After breakfast, we all get dressed and grab some books to head out farther on the property and get a few photos in the woods. The blue SUV from earlier has disappeared from the driveway next door, and I can't help wondering where they might've gone.

"You good?" Memphis asks, walking into my line of vision as we cross the yard. I hadn't realized I'd stopped to stare at the house until I notice that he's leaving me.

"Yeah, I'm fine." My voice sounds as tired as I feel.

He looks as if he doesn't believe me but doesn't bother pressing the issue. "Listen, about earlier—"

"You don't have to say anything. I promise I'm letting it go."

"I was talking about when we were in the house," he says, bumping my hand with his.

"Oh."

"I just...I want you to know that I'm here, you know," he says eventually. "And not just because I have... Not just because I... Not for any particular reason other than because I want you to be okay."

I glance up at him, squinting in the sun. "Because you're madly in love with me and ridiculously attracted to me?" I tease, brushing his hip with mine. When I do, he stops walking, takes hold of my hip, his hand pressed

135

against my back, and spins me around to face him, the look on his face as shocked as I feel. "What are you doing?"

He lets out a breath. "I have no idea."

For a moment, we just stand there, bodies pressed together, eyes dancing between each other's and our lips.

"I don't know how to do this," he says softly.

"What are you trying to do?"

He opens his mouth to answer, but before he can say anything, the sound of tires on the gravel road behind us causes everyone to freeze. Memphis releases me, and I pull away. When I turn around to see where the sound has come from, something cold grips my organs.

The familiar black sedan pulls into the driveway, and I know—I just know—he's back.

"Lena," Memphis whispers.

"I know."

It takes several minutes for anything to happen. For a while, the car just idles, and I hold my breath. Then, it shuts off. The headlights go out, and the driver's door opens.

I bite my lower lip, picking at the skin around my thumbnail as I wait. Then, it happens. The man steps from the front seat, and I feel Memphis grab my arm, prepared to hold me back.

"We have to call the police," I say, keeping my voice low as everyone gathers around me.

"What's going on?" Austin asks.

"That's the man," Memphis answers for me, keeping us hidden in the treeline.

"The man from last night?" Logan asks. "The one who..."

He trails off, but before he can finish the question,

everything stops. The entire world tilts on its axis, throwing us down so we bang our heads so hard we hallucinate. That's the only possible explanation. Because next, the passenger door of the car opens, and a brown head of hair rises from that side.

No.

No.

No.

It's impossible, but as she turns to face us, I know it's true. It's her, but it can't be her. Memphis glances at me, and I don't have to meet his eyes to sense the betrayal there. He thinks I've lied. He thinks I'm crazy.

The woman I watched die last night is standing a hundred yards away, alive and well.

CHAPTER FIFTEEN

"Lena, wait!" Memphis shouts, running after me, but I don't care. I can't stop. I feel like I'm losing my mind, like I can't trust myself anymore. Like no one should trust me. I need to know the truth.

Is it really possible I imagined everything I saw? I know I thought the man was dangerous even before the incident last night, but this feels ridiculous.

The couple is crossing their driveway toward the porch when I approach them. Their eyes widen like frightened cats. I can't blame them. I look as unhinged as I feel, I'm sure.

I'm out of breath when I speak. "You... You're okay?"

The woman looks at the man, whom I can only assume to be her husband, then back at me. "Excuse me?"

The group catches up to us, and I hear their tired breaths behind me, though none of them say anything.

"Who are you?" the man asks.

"I... We're staying next door." I refuse to look at the man. Instead, I keep eye contact with his wife, speaking only to her. "I thought you were hurt last night. I called the police to help you, but you were gone."

"What are you talking about?" the woman demands, her nose wrinkling.

I blink. The betrayal stings as real as a slap to the cheek. "I saw you. It looked like there was blood all over you. On your arms and your hair...and your shirt."

"Last night?" She shakes her head. "Impossible. We weren't home last night."

"You were," I argue. "I saw you." A dull ache is forming in my temple, and I can feel my pulse pounding in my head as if it's a warning. *Run, run. Run, run. Run, run.*

The man steps in front of his wife, his eyes dark and guarded. "Like my wife just told you, you're wrong. We were out of town last night."

"Who are you?" Memphis asks, moving closer to me. "We spoke to the owners after the police contacted them. You're not supposed to be here."

"What are you talking about?" the man demands, looking back at his wife. "The police were here? At our house?"

"Yes, along with the *real* homeowners, who said no one else is supposed to be here," Memphis repeats pointedly.

The man gives a breathless laugh of disbelief. "Look, I'm not trying to be rude, but I have no idea what you're talking about, and I don't think you possibly can either. *We're* the homeowners." He pats his fingers against his chest, then gestures toward his wife.

The wife who's very much alive.

The wife whom I watched die.

My head hurts.

I'm so utterly confused.

"Impossible," Memphis says.

"I assure you it isn't, and frankly, it's none of your business or concern."

"But...you can't be the owners," I say under my breath. "The owners were just here. We talked to them."

"She's right," Memphis agrees.

"What owners?" he asks, exasperated. "Look, I have no idea what you're talking about, but we need to get inside." He glances over at the door, and his face goes ghastly white. "Oh my god, the door... The door. *Are you kidding me?*" Both hands go to the side of his head. "I'm going to have to call the sheriff's department and see what's going on. Come on. Get in the house."

He puts a hand behind his wife's back and leads her inside, casting an accusatory glance our way before slamming the door, though he seems to have forgotten it's broken and doesn't latch. I turn back to look at the rest of the group.

"Well, at least you know she's okay now," Mara says with an apologetic shrug. "That's a good thing, right?"

I nod. "Yeah, I guess. But, I mean, how is that possible? What the heck is going on?"

To that, no one seems to have an answer. When I look at Memphis, he's shaking his head with a puzzled look on his face.

"Ethan sure picked a quiet little town, didn't he?" Austin jokes.

CHAPTER SIXTEEN

Back inside, I head upstairs to my room and call Officer Montgomery on the number he contacted me from last night.

"Montgomery."

"Hi, Officer Montgomery. This is Lena Ortega from the house on Buchanan Street last night. You told me I could call you back on this number if there were any issues."

"Yes, Ms. Ortega. That's right. What can I do for you?"

"Um, so, a couple showed up at the house this morning claiming to be the owners, and they said they'd spoken with you and had to cut their vacation short to come home and deal with this. But then they left at some point, and now the first couple is back and saying *they* are the owners. And the woman from last night is here and apparently fine."

"So, the woman you thought you saw get killed is at the house now?"

"Yes."

"And she hasn't been harmed? She's fine?"

"Right. That's how it seems."

He's quiet for a beat. "Okay, then, I guess I'm not understanding what the problem is."

"Um." My mouth goes dry. "Nothing, I guess. But there are two couples saying they own this house."

"Well, until one of the owners calls to file a complaint with us, that's not really our problem. And it's certainly not yours. If no one is hurt, then, as far as the law is concerned, our work here is done."

I swallow. "Don't you want to come check on her or something?"

"Why would I? You just said yourself she's fine, and we told you yesterday there were no signs she wouldn't be."

I want to point out that they also told me yesterday there were no signs she existed, and here's the living, breathing proof she does, but instead, I say nothing. I'm too angry. Too confused and upset.

"Is there anything else I can do for you?" Officer Montgomery asks. "I need to get back to work."

Shame swells in my chest. I shake my head, though he can't see me. "No, that was all."

"Have a nice day, Ms. Ortega."

He ends the call before I have the chance to. Slowly, I lower the phone down from my ear.

"What did he say?" Mara asks, and I jump, turning around to see all of my housemates standing in the doorway, watching me nervously. Maybe they're scared I'm losing it, too. If the situation were reversed, I probably would be.

I lick my lips, shoving my phone in my pocket and trying to act as if nothing's wrong. "Nothing. They aren't going to do anything unless one of the supposed owners calls and reports it. Otherwise, they're pretty much saying the case is closed."

"Even though you told them there are two different people claiming to live there?" Memphis asks.

"Well, they're kind of right," Logan says, opening a small closet upstairs and pulling out the broom, then carefully sweeping the hallway as he speaks. "I mean, whatever's going on with the house, it's not like it affects us. At least we know no one died. That's the most important thing, right?"

"It's still really weird," Paulette says, twisting her foot in place.

"Yeah, totally," he agrees, sweeping the small pile of dust into a dustpan. He disappears into the hallway bathroom and returns a moment later, connecting the dustpan to the broom and placing it back inside the closet.

My housemates' eyes scan the space, landing everywhere but on me. No one seems to know what to say.

"Maybe I should just go home. I'm sorry. I know I'm not being much fun this weekend." I rest my chin against my chest, feeling new tears stinging my eyes.

"You can't go home," Mara says. "Girl, please. Don't let whatever's going on next door ruin this weekend. We're still here to have fun. Just...I don't know, just think of it like a mystery. That's what we like best, isn't it?" She claps her hands together and puffs out her bottom lip. "Please? You wouldn't leave your very best friend, would you? It's our last chance to see each other for who knows how long. Besides, we're strong, capable women, and I will kick anyone's ass who tries to mess with you." She wags a finger at the men. "And that goes for you guys, too."

"She's right," Austin says, stepping forward. "You have to stay. Come on. It's our last night. Let's make the best of it."

I look at Memphis, who's being strangely quiet, seemingly lost in thought.

"Look, we probably can't get flights out tonight anyway," Paulette says. "We're leaving tomorrow. Less than twenty-four hours. Why spend the next few hours in the stress of trying to change flights and get a ride to the airport —wondering if you'll make it in time—if you don't have to? Just hang out with us and have fun. We don't want you to go."

Austin pulls out his phone. "It's true. I mean, the chance of getting a flight out tonight is slim. We could maybe get a hotel or something, if you wanted to try that just so we didn't have to stay here, but it seems kind of drastic when nothing's happened to any of us. Whatever you saw, the woman is clearly fine." The corner of his mouth tips up with a grin. "Maybe it was some weird sex thing."

"Do you want to leave, Lena? No one is going to stop you," Memphis says firmly, and that one sentence becomes a challenge. Because he's right. I could leave if I wanted to. But if I do, I give up on everything I wanted this weekend to be.

"Hey, guys," Austin says, wagging his phone in the air.

"You're not going to want to leave now. Look who's coming after all."

On his screen is a message from Ethan.

> You still up for some company? Flying in tonight. I'll be there around seven.

CHAPTER SEVENTEEN

The news that Ethan is on his way has everyone in better spirits, myself included. To pass the time and keep ourselves occupied, we gather in the living room with a board game we've found in one of the cabinets in the house.

Quite fittingly, the game is Clue, a murder mystery game that was one of my favorites as a child.

Paulette brings in a box of spiked seltzer. "Last night, guys. Drink up. You have the choice between mango and lime, and there's only one right answer." She plops down on the ground, cracking open a can of the mango-flavored drink.

"So, next time"—Austin moves his purple game piece across the board before grabbing a lime seltzer from the box —"I vote we visit a beach."

"Us two and three!" Paulette cries, lifting Logan's hand with hers. She moves so quickly she bumps into the game board, sending pieces flying. "Oops. Sorry."

"Oh no!" Mara cries.

Everyone moves quickly to reset the board, trying to remember where their pieces had been last.

Once everything looks like we think it should, we take turns each choosing a seltzer from the box.

"Oh, I'm obsessed with this lime! How can you possibly think mango is better?" Mara asks, kissing the side of the can before cracking it open.

"Uh, because I'm not a monster," Paulette says.

"Fair enough. More for me." She takes a drink, wiping her mouth with the back of her hand. "So, obviously, this hasn't been the trip we all imagined, but I'm glad we're doing this. This game. This last night to try and find some normalcy. I'm so happy I got to meet you guys." Her voice is somber. "Ignoring all the weird stuff, this has still been fun, right?" she asks. "The dinners and the drinks and the pictures. Plus the shopping." She wiggles her shoulders halfheartedly, trying to convince us.

Seeing that she needs me the way I've needed her this weekend, I nod. "Yeah, it has," I agree, hoping I sound convincing. "Thank you all for helping me through a weird weekend, but also just a weird time in my life in general. I'm not sure I could've made it through this last year without you, and definitely not this weekend."

"What are friends for?" Mara asks, blowing me a kiss. "And, hey, it wouldn't be a thriller book lovers' get-together without a little mystery, would it? It's going to make for an interesting story, if nothing else." She winks at Paulette. "Something to tell the grandkids about, right?"

Paulette kisses the air. "Of course, darling."

Mara hums a tune as she moves her piece into place.

"You know, if we could solve it, it would actually make

an interesting story," Austin says playfully, tapping his chin. "A book. Like, we could write it and make millions or something. Or, you know, hire a ghostwriter."

"To write about what? The mystery?" I ask. "About next door?"

"Sure. If we could solve it, it would make a cool story."

Slowly, heads start to turn around the circle as we all look to gauge each other's reactions. To my surprise, the idea isn't shot down right away. Suddenly, with the panic and the chaos having died down, the group seems more receptive to trying to figure this all out.

"Seriously, guys, what else do we have to do for the next few hours?" Austin asks. "We all spend our days doing this: solving mysteries and picking up clues. If anyone should be good at it, it's us." He seems more hyped about the decision now as he shifts to sit on his knees. "Come on. Let's run through some theories. What could be going on next door? No idea is a bad one." He waves his hand in the air, encouraging us to tell him our ideas.

"Maybe it was all a prank," Memphis says, his voice hesitant. "The woman we talked to earlier said she told her husband they were going to have problems when they started renting this out to random people. Maybe they set it all up to scare us off so we'd leave a bad review or something. Deter others from coming here."

"Oooh, solid theory," Austin says. "My thoughts"—he puts his hands up into a square shape as if holding a picture frame—"what if...she just had a red stain on her shirt and tripped?"

Everyone laughs, and he seems quite pleased with himself.

"It still doesn't explain the two separate couples both claiming to be the owners," Mara points out.

"And the blood was on her hands, arms, and head, too, not just her shirt," I remind him.

"Fair enough." Austin winks at us. "Okay." He clicks his tongue, tapping his chin. "Oh, I know! Maybe it's a timeshare thing."

"Oh! Oh! That's good!" Paulette hops up and down on her knees from her seat on the floor. "And maybe the police called the wrong people."

"A timeshare in Bumfuck, Nowhere?" Memphis asks with a scowl. "I don't think that's how that works."

"Why don't we ask one of the other neighbors?" Paulette says.

"Ask them what?" Mara looks at her, her dark brows drawn down.

"Ask them who lives there. There's a house down the road that we passed on our way downtown the other day. We could stop by and ask them which of the couples actually lives there. It's a small town. Everyone knows their neighbor and all that jazz." She waves a hand in the air. "It's worth a shot."

Austin claps his hands together, jumping up to his feet. "Eh? Eh? That's the energy I'm talking about! We're taking this little detective show on the road." He adjusts the neck of his shirt as if it's a collar.

"Wait, are you serious? We're just going to go and...*ask* the neighbors?" Mara asks with a scowl. "As in ring the doorbell and be like, 'Hey, we're total strangers, but we think you could help us out'? Just like that? What if they're dangerous?"

149

"I'll keep you safe," Austin teases, wrapping his arms around her waist.

She pulls away from him, slapping his chest playfully. "Yeah, right. More like you'd need *me* to protect *you*."

"I'm in," I say, thankful to have them finally interested in what's going on here in any capacity.

"Yeah? Who else?" Austin asks, raising his hand.

Memphis's hand rises slowly, then Paulette's and Logan's. Mara is the last to agree, but eventually, we're all on board.

"Alright, cool. Get your coats, kiddies. We're hittin' the road," Austin calls, rubbing his hands together.

We head for the foyer, where our coats are still hanging up from our trip to the woods earlier. I'm only just now realizing we never took the photos we were planning to. The commotion with the neighbors—or potentially fake neighbors—ruined that, among so many other things.

"Can you hand me mine?" Paulette asks Logan, who is all too happy to oblige.

"Everyone ready?" Austin asks when we're all bundled up.

"I guess," Mara groans, looking less than pleased with our plans. With our coats and shoes on, we make our way to the back door.

Outside, the evening air is already cooler than last night, and I wrap myself up in my coat with a shiver, my fingers burning from the cold. I place my hands in my pockets, trying to warm them up.

Memphis stays next to me, with Mara on the other side. Paulette, Logan, and Austin lead the way, skipping and holding hands and generally being silly as we go. To them, this is still all just a game, but to me, it feels like so much more.

The world around us is quiet as we move down the dimly lit street, the only sounds are an owl hooting in a tree somewhere in the woods, the sound of gravel crunching under our shoes, and the occasional car passing by on a nearby road—close enough to hear but not to see.

When we round the curve, the small house Paulette mentioned comes into view. It's the nearest one, but still quite a walk away from the two houses. The house is small and quaint—a single-story, ranch-style building with a tiny front porch illuminated by a dim porch light.

We approach the front door cautiously, searching for a doorbell camera, but there doesn't seem to be one. Austin lifts his hand to knock on the door, and suddenly, I worry this is a terrible idea.

What if Mara was right? We could get shot doing this. Killed. We'd barely make the headlines in a world where that happens all too often.

What if these people aren't friendly?

What if they warn the neighbors we were asking about them?

What if they call the police?

The door swings open relatively quickly, and an older woman—probably my parents' age, I'd guess—greets us. "Well, hello." She looks around the house outside as if checking for a car or a problem. "Is everything alright?" I catch a hint of fear in her eyes as she grips the door tighter, taking a barely noticeable step back.

"Sorry to bother you so late, ma'am," Austin says,

laying on the charm. "We're staying just up over the hill in the big house." He points toward it.

"Oh, yes. Okay. Has something happened?"

"No, no. Everything's fine. We just wondered if you knew anything about the people who live next door to it?"

She presses her lips together, her eyes bouncing between each of us. "Well, I don't—"

"What's going on?" A short, older man with a round belly walks up behind her, interrupting whatever she was about to say.

She pats his chest. "Honey, these kids are staying up in the old Buchanan house. They're asking about the neighbors. It's alright."

"What about the neighbors?" the man asks, one bushy, gray eyebrow shooting up toward his receding hairline.

"There was a sort of...disturbance," Austin says, choosing his words carefully. "Last night. And we're a little freaked out. We were just hoping you could tell us if they're...okay. You know, normal. Safe."

"Well, I'm afraid we don't know much about them, to be honest," the woman says finally. "A younger couple lives there. A man and a woman. No kids. But we've only seen them in passing. They aren't around much, and when they are, they tend to keep to themselves."

"Could you describe them to us?" Memphis asks.

The woman seems to ponder the question. "Um, I'd say midforties?" She looks to her husband, who confirms with a nod. "She's tall and thin with red hair, and he has black curly hair, but he's usually wearing a ball cap. He's shorter, kind of stocky."

They're describing the second couple we met. The ones who claimed they had just returned from a vacation.

"Do you ever see anyone else there?" Austin asks. "At the house? Maybe a cleaner or a house sitter?"

"Can't say that I have," she says, looking again at her husband. "But we don't get out much. Besides, there's no real reason to be up that way"—she shoves her thumb to her right—"when town is this way." Her thumb swings over, pointing to her left.

"We understand," he says, pressing his hands together into a prayer motion. "Thanks so much for talking to us. You guys have a great night."

We walk away from the house with more questions swirling in my mind. If the second couple was telling the truth, who is the first couple? And what happened to the woman? Why did she have blood on her shirt? And why would she lie? She has to be afraid of the man. Maybe she knew he would hurt her if she confirmed my story. Or hurt me.

"We know who the real neighbors are now, so we just have to figure out who the others are, and then we've solved it," Austin announces to the group as if he's really cracked something.

The truth is, even if we figure out who the other people are, I'm not sure it will tell us anything. We still don't know what they're doing in that house, how they got in there, or what was happening the night the man attacked the woman.

"We should try to look up the address," Paulette says. "Maybe there's a record of people who have lived there before."

153

"But I doubt there'd be a record of these people who are essentially breaking in and squatting," Mara points out.

As we walk back up the hill, Memphis pulls his phone out with a sudden look of determination.

"What are you doing?" I ask, leaning over to see his phone screen. I'm probably breaking some sort of rule in terms of checking the phone of someone who might like you and might've almost kissed you earlier, but I don't care at the moment.

"Trying to see if there are any reports of crime around here, but I'm not really seeing anything." He pauses, twisting his mouth and scrolling down farther on his screen. "Man, for a small town, a lot of people go missing."

My heart sinks. "What do you mean?" As he continues to scroll, I see that he's right. Just on the first page, there are five articles about people who've gone missing.

"Do they all match a certain profile?" I ask, not sure how this could be relevant to our current mystery but intrigued nonetheless. I think back to what Bertie at the bookstore said. *This may be a sleepy little small town, but we've got our problems just like everywhere else.*

"I don't think it's anything to worry about," he says, shoving his phone back into his pocket. "Just a few disappearances. Nothing involving the house, just the town in general. Anyway, it was only a theory, but it's a dead end."

Try as he might to assure me, I suspect he's lying. I just don't know why.

CHAPTER EIGHTEEN

On our way back up the street and toward the house, I get an idea.

A really, really bad idea, but also the only one we've had since we left the little house at the end of the street. Slowly, theories and suggestions for things to try next have died out, and we've reverted to talk of what we'll do once Ethan arrives and how we'll explain to him all that he's missed.

With this new idea in mind, I jog ahead of the group and cross the street. Double-checking that no one is outside the house, I move closer.

"Where are you going?" Austin calls.

"Shhh!" I warn, waving a hand at him to get him to keep it down. "Something Paulette said earlier gave me an idea. She mentioned looking up records of people who have lived here." I check the house once more, then close my eyes, approach the mailbox, and tear it open. "What if we can find a name on their mail?" The first two items inside are junk mail addressed to the current resident with no actual name.

"What?" Paulette whisper-yells.

"What the hell are you doing?" Memphis demands, moving to stand next to me. "Are you trying to get arrested?"

"Of course not. I just want to find out their name. Then we can look them up and—"

"And go to prison?" He shuts the mailbox, standing in front of it and refusing to budge. "This is illegal, Lena. Nothing matters enough to do this."

"It's only illegal if I open their mail," I say, though I don't really know if that's true.

"No." He shakes his head, crossing his arms. "Absolutely not. I'm not letting you do this."

"I'm not asking permission," I huff, trying to shove him out of the way.

"He's right, Lena," Mara says, resting a hand on my shoulder. "We should go. It's too risky."

"I—"

"What the hell is going on out here?" The man's angry voice tears through the air. "What are you doing by my mailbox?"

Memphis spins around, blocking me. "Just walking past." He grabs my arm, pulling me forward. "Have a good night."

"I'm going to call the police if I see you around here again. Stay on your property and away from mine," he says, watching as we walk toward our house.

I hang my head, rage coursing through me.

It doesn't matter, though. Not really.

I wanted to check every piece of mail, but one was better than nothing. I got a name, and that's what matters.

Once we're inside, I slip away from the group and look him up.

Samuel Hawthorne. Fulfield, Kentucky.

I scroll through several results before I find the right one, but when I do, it's every bit of confirmation that I needed. Just like the neighbors down the road told us. The second couple, the one on vacation, they're the ones who live in this house. The ones who own it. And now we have a name: Samuel and Elizabeth Hawthorne.

Whoever is there right now, whoever is claiming to be the owners, are liars, and probably dangerous.

I don't know what to do with the information, though. Briefly, I consider calling the police, but they've made it clear they won't help unless the actual owner calls to report this. The other problem is that I don't know where the *actual* owners are. Samuel and Elizabeth left the house after their brief visit this morning, and they have yet to return.

An email comes across my screen about checking out tomorrow, and, based on the sounds of their phones buzzing, everyone else seems to get the same email around the time I do.

I close out of mine, still focused on trying to reach Samuel. A few of the sites list phone numbers, but none of them match any of the others, and I suspect they're all wrong. And even if I did call, how in the world would I explain myself? It isn't like we got off on a great foot this morning, and I still don't know who the people next door are, but at least maybe I could tell them they're there and they should come home and—

"Um, guys?" Memphis says from where he's standing near the window in the living room.

"Yeah?" I ask, looking up with worry at the tone of his voice. Something is wrong.

"Did you all get the checkout email just now?"

By now, everyone is staring at him.

"What? Do they want us to do some weird amount of cleaning or something?" Logan asks.

"Oh my god. I once had a host who asked me to sweep and mop all the floors, take out the trash, start a load of laundry, do all my dishes, and still charged me a three-hundred-dollar cleaning fee on top of it," Paulette chimes in. "Talk about a scam."

"No," he says, looking directly at me. "Er, well, maybe, but it's not that. They, um, the owners..." He turns his phone around so I can see the screen. "It's them, Lena."

I stare at the photos on his phone screen, two faces inside two separate circles, under the words **Your Hosts.**

It's them. The couple next door.

CHAPTER NINETEEN

"You guys, if they're the owners, they'll have keys to this house," Paulette says, standing up from her seat on the couch. "That means they could come in here in the middle of the night."

She doesn't need to elaborate further. We all understand.

"We need to leave," I say firmly, thinking back to the noise Memphis and I heard in the house in the middle of the night when everyone else was still in their rooms. Could it have been them? Could they have been in the house? "We need to leave right now."

"But what about Ethan?" Austin asks. "He's on his way here. Shouldn't we wait for him? Or try to warn him somehow?"

I check the clock. It's just after seven. He should be arriving any minute, but we don't have time to wait. "Send him a message and tell him we're leaving. Tell him not to come here."

Austin looks at Mara, who seems to be in agreement as she nods and starts to leave the room.

"She's right. He shouldn't come here. It's not safe for any of us. I'm going to get my things, and we need to go," she says.

"I'll get us a ride." In an instant, I have my rideshare app open and am booking the trip to the airport. We'll figure out what to do from there.

Everyone jumps into action then, realizing this is serious and happening now. I rush to my room and throw my things into my bag, my body pulsing with adrenaline. Everything about this feels wrong. How could we have not known?

In truth, after Ethan booked this place, I hardly paid attention to the emails aside from getting the code to get inside the house. Nothing else mattered.

Besides, even if I'd seen their photos in the emails, the chances I'd recognize them in person without knowing where I'd seen them before are slim.

How many times have they come in here? Could they have cameras hidden in this house? What sort of game are they playing with us? Could they be trying to get us to leave so they get free money for our stay?

It has to be something else, but I just can't see what.

And why would the owners next door allow them to stay there and then lie to us about it?

With our bags packed—and without doing any of the cleaning items on their list—we make our way to the foyer and wait for our ride to arrive.

"I hate this so much," Mara whispers, her voice low and teary.

"We're getting out of here," Logan says, pulling Paulette into his side with a kiss to the top of her head. "That's what matters."

I notice she's changed into a new shirt. This one has Dolly Parton riding a winged opossum over a Waffle House. Despite our circumstances, it makes me laugh, and that feels strange to me.

This weekend feels like it's lasted a year, and I haven't laughed or smiled the entire time.

Memphis moves closer to me, his arm brushing mine, his finger looping with my pinkie for just a second. "What time are they supposed to get here?"

I check the app, hoping my cheeks aren't as red as they feel. "Another fifteen minutes."

"We have time for a group photo then," Paulette says. "At least one."

"Oh, good idea," Logan says.

We huddle together, and I pull out my phone, snapping a selfie of the six of us. I'm not sure I'll ever be able to look at this photo without remembering how I'm feeling in this moment—confused and terrified more than anything else.

"Have you heard from Ethan yet?" Paulette asks Austin. "I'd hate for him to get here after we leave, but shouldn't he have been here by now?"

Austin checks his phone and shakes his head. "Nothing yet. Maybe his flight was delayed."

"Did you check it?" I ask.

"I don't have the number."

Just then, my phone begins vibrating, and I look down to see a call coming in from our driver. "It's our driver. Everyone, *shhh*." I place the phone to my ear. "Hello?"

"Um, hi. It's Darren, your driver. We, uh, we have a problem." He sounds oddly entertained by this problem.

My stomach drops. "What do you mean?"

"I'm trying to get to you, but there's a tree down in the middle of the road I need to take."

"Can't you go another way?"

"It's the road you're on. Buchanan. There's no way around." He sighs. "I'm sorry. I'm going to have to cancel the ride."

"No, wait!" I shout. Everyone around me moves closer. "How far away are you?"

"I'm at the cross street of Buchanan. But as soon as I try to turn onto it, the road is completely blocked." He sounds as stressed as I feel.

"So, you're just at the end of the road? We can walk to you. Can you stay where you are if we come to you?" I clutch the phone with both hands.

"I can't wait around all night," he says hesitantly. "I can give you maybe twenty minutes to get here, but I have to get home before my wife leaves for work to watch our son."

"We'll get there. Please...please don't leave us. It's an emergency."

"You have twenty minutes," he says. "At twenty-one minutes, though, I have to go. I'm sorry. There's no way I can push the timeline like that."

"We'll be there." I end the call and look at the others. "There's a tree down in the road. He can't get to us. He's willing to wait twenty minutes, but we have to hurry." I pull the handle of my suitcase up, rolling it toward the door.

"Wait, we're going to walk?" Austin asks. "It's already dark. How do we know it's safe?"

"We don't, but it's just up the road. Come on. There's not much time."

I turn around to see no one following me at first. Then, Mara grabs her bags and moves toward me. Memphis is next to follow, and soon we're all on our way out the door. We don't bother locking it—who would we really be locking out anyway?—as we head out across the yard and down the road.

The neighbor's driveway is empty, which makes me feel only slightly better. Wherever they've gone, there's a great chance they'll be back soon.

I pick up my pace, moving faster when something catches my eye. Parked back behind the house is the blue SUV from this morning. The one that belongs to the Hawthornes. I must've missed it earlier.

I stop, despite not wanting to waste time, something roiling in my stomach. Why on earth would the Hawthornes still be here? Why would their car be parked in the grass, toward the tree line, as if it's meant to be hidden?

In the dark, it nearly is.

Could they be in on it together? Both sets of supposed owners?

"What's wrong?" Mara asks.

"It's the SUV from this morning," Memphis answers before I can as if he knows my every thought. "The people who own the house."

"They're here?" Austin asks.

"I don't know," I say, trying to think.

"We need to go," Memphis reminds me. "Come on. We're wasting time."

"Hey. What do you think's down here?" Austin asks, drawing our attention to a cellar door in the ground up against the house.

"I don't know, but I don't think I want to know," Paulette whines.

"Come on, guys. We need to go," Logan says, dragging her backward. "We're going to miss our ride. The neighbors could come home at any minute."

Memphis takes a step back, but I can't move.

I'm pinned firmly in place as Mara studies me. "Lena?"

"We're not going to make it to the car anyway," Austin points out. "Even running, it's at least thirty minutes to the end of the road, and we all have our bags slowing us down. I thought you wanted to solve the mystery."

"Fuck the mystery," Paulette says. "We have to try to make it to the car. Come on, you guys. Seriously."

"Lena, let's go," Memphis agrees, snapping his fingers. "We're wasting time. This is none of our business."

"They could be hurt," I say, nausea overwhelming me. I suddenly feel dizzy. "The Hawthornes. They could be down there. Or in the house somewhere. We have to check." I would hope someone would check on me, that someone would care enough to try to help.

Memphis is staring at me as if I've started speaking a foreign language and I realize I don't think I ever told them who the Hawthornes are. "*Who?* Look, we have to go. We'll call the police from the car."

"Because they believed us so well last time?" I stare at him, shaking my head.

"They weren't even nice to you, Lena. And now you're willing to risk your life for them?" He sets his jaw, clearly furious with me.

I don't expect him to understand why I can't walk away. I'm not even sure *I* understand it.

"They're still people. If this man is dangerous, if he has his wife living in terror, how do we know he didn't hurt them? Maybe they came home and confronted them and..." I can't bear to voice my worst thoughts. "Please. I need to do this. I need to understand what's going on."

Memphis looks like he's going to argue, but I turn away.

"Feel free to go if you need to. I won't ask you to stay," I whisper. "But I am."

Austin nods, needing no further instruction. "Someone help me with the door, will you?" He takes hold of it, lifting with a groan.

"Guys, we aren't waiting," Paulette says, already almost too far away to hear. I look over my shoulder to see her and Logan running down the road. I don't want to split up, but it seems I'm being given no choice. I check with Memphis, who looks like he'd rather be doing anything but this, though he doesn't budge.

Mara helps Austin pull the door to the cellar open, and the second he does, I know what we'll find.

The scent reaches my nose even from where I stand— rotting flesh. Decay. Death.

Mara covers her mouth, coughing, and Austin turns away, fanning his face.

"Oh god," Mara whines.

My knees are suddenly weak. "We need to call the police."

"Did they kill them?" Mara asks, refusing to look. "They killed them, didn't they?"

I step toward the cellar, my nose and mouth tucked into the elbow of my shirt. I try to look inside, but the smell is so strong it burns my eyes. I can't breathe. Can't think.

"It can't be them," I say softly, so low I'm not sure anyone heard me.

Whatever this smell is, there's no way this is from just the last few hours. I don't know much about dead bodies, but I know enough to know this has been here for at least a day. Maybe it's only a dead animal.

Even as I try to force my brain to believe it, I know I can't.

The sight of her bloody shirt in the window flashes in my mind.

Is she a twin? Did he somehow trick me into believing she was alive? Was her body here all this time? Did I fail her?

I suck in a sharp breath and flip on the light on my phone, leaning down into the cellar and searching for the source of the smell.

Sources.

I scramble backward, my body going numb as my vision lands on the three sets of eyes staring back at me. Lifeless and empty, but haunting nonetheless.

"What is it?" Austin asks from where he stands at a safe distance.

Memphis is right behind me, catching me when I stumble. He takes the phone and looks inside. I hope he'll say

I'm seeing things. That the police were right. That I've lost my mind.

Anything would be better than this. Insanity included.

But when he turns around, I know he's going to confirm my worst fear.

He runs a hand over his face and turns off my flashlight, looking down.

"What?" Mara demands in hysterics.

"No," I beg him. "It's not possible. Please, no."

He shakes his head, pulling out his phone and lifting it to his ear. He passes my phone back to me. "I'm calling the police. You should go to the car, Lena. Run and catch up with Paulette. I'll wait here."

"Calling the police? What? Why? What did you see? Is it them? What's down there?" Austin asks, stepping forward.

"It's the couple from this morning." Memphis swallows, then lifts his head to meet Austin's eyes. "And...and Ethan."

CHAPTER TWENTY

"What? No!" Mara cries, covering her mouth. "No, it can't be him. It can't be Ethan. He was supposed to be here. He was supposed to be okay."

From where he stands, Austin staggers. "How? Is this a joke? Is this some shitty joke?" He shoves past Memphis to look for himself, and I know the moment he sees him because his knees buckle, and he falls to the ground. He's on his hands and knees, wailing and banging his fists on the ground.

Everything seems to be happening in slow motion but also at warp speed. My knees give out, and I fall to the ground, just like Austin did, bile filling my throat. As I listen to Memphis on the phone with 911, I hyperventilate, sure I'm going to pass out at any moment. When he ends the call, I bend at the waist, puking up the contents of my stomach.

I can't breathe.

I can't breathe.

I can't breathe.

"He can't be dead," I mumble, more to myself than anything. "He can't be. It's not possible. He's alive. He's alive because we just talked to him. He...he has to be alive."

"They must've found him when he came tonight." Austin wipes his eyes with the back of his arm. "That's why he never got here. That's why he was late."

"He was supposed to be okay," Mara whispers. "He has to be okay."

"They didn't do this tonight. He's been dead longer than a few minutes," Memphis says, and I silently agree. Something about this isn't right.

Aside from the obvious.

"What do you mean?" Austin asks, struggling to stand up.

"He's, um, h-he's been there for a while." Memphis's voice is shaky as he squeezes his eyes shut, thinking. Calculating, maybe. "Several hours, at least. Probably more like a day or two."

"How would you know?" Denial draws a wrinkle across Austin's forehead. "That's impossible. We were just talking to him."

Memphis's eyes pop open. "I read a lot of nonfiction, remember? True crime. There's no way his body would look like that after just a few minutes." He runs a hand across his mouth, shaking his head. "He's been here at least a day. Has to have been."

"If that's the case, who's been messaging us? If he's been dead for a day or longer, who has his phone?" Austin looks around as if accusing us.

"Days... Maybe that's why he canceled. Maybe he was... Maybe he was gone all along," Mara whimpers, looking at me with horror in her eyes. She chews her bottom lip, her chin quivering.

What if that's why he never texted me back?

But then who was messaging us on his profile?

I can't seem to swallow. My throat is tight and uncomfortable. I'm not sure I'm breathing.

"If they killed him, they probably have his phone," Austin says, running a hand through his hair. "We have to get back to the house and lock the door. Wait for the police to come."

"The operator said it'll be at least half an hour before someone can make it out here," Memphis informs us. "And that's not including whatever time it takes them to get around or deal with the tree in the road. Even under the best conditions, these people have the house key. Locking the doors won't do any good and it's too long to wait. We have to run." His eyes go wide. "Oh, shit. We have to warn Paulette and Logan."

I swallow as reality sets in. Poor Paulette and Logan are running down the road with no idea what's happened.

"He's right. We have to run. Right now, our only chance of getting away from these people is getting out of this town," I say, standing to my feet. "We don't know when they'll be back. We've told the police about the... bodies." As I say the word, his face flashes in my mind. He was a person. Someone with thoughts and feelings and goals and ambitions. He had people who cared about him. And now, in the blink of an eye, he's gone. Reduced to rotting in the dirt under a house. *I'm so sorry, Ethan. So, so sorry.* "Now, we have to get out of here."

"Will we even make it?" Mara asks, already moving.

We all race to keep up. *We just have to try*, I tell her silently, not willing to expend my energy on any more words. *We just have to try.*

My legs burn as much as my lungs, but I refuse to quit moving as my feet slam into the ground beneath me. My bag drags across the gravel, the wheels bumping and jostling it in every direction, but I can't slow down.

I can't.

I won't.

Memphis stays with me, though I suspect he's moving slower than he is capable of in order to stay together.

Guilt weighs on me for letting us split up in the first place. Paulette and Logan are in danger now, and we may not make it to warn them. We were safer in a group.

Safety in numbers.

Though I know, realistically, it wasn't my fault, and the group's safety isn't my responsibility, I wish I'd asked them to stay. I'd been so determined to find out why the Hawthornes' SUV was there, I hadn't really been paying attention to what was happening with everyone else. I wish I'd told them we shouldn't split up. I wish I'd asked them to consider staying.

And then there's Ethan.

Sweet, kind, funny Ethan. The Ethan I've spent the weekend feeling betrayed by. Angry that he hadn't answered my messages. Hurt that he'd missed this without so much as a message to say he was sorry or to tell me he was hurting.

The Ethan who, just a few days ago, I hoped I stood a chance with, saw a possible future with.

Now, in the blink of an eye, that's all gone.

And for what? What exactly is going on?

We still have no idea.

When we reach the end of the road, I see the tree the man was talking about, but Paulette and Logan are nowhere to be seen. Maybe that means they reached the car. Maybe that means they got away.

I hope and pray that's true.

"Where are they?" Mara asks, out of breath and panting.

I check my phone and see it's been forty-one minutes since he gave us twenty. If they reached the car, they're long gone. For their sake, I hope they made it in time, and this town is already starting to become a distant memory.

I hope they're somewhere safe. That they'll send help for us. Go to the police station or the airport and demand someone come and remove this tree.

But that will be an hour from now, which means we're in even more danger with no hope for rescue coming soon.

"They could've gone into the woods," Austin says, a hand on his chest as he struggles to catch his breath.

"But which way?" I ask, looking at the woods on either side of the road. "We have to catch up to them and warn them."

"Someone try to call them," Austin says, pulling out his phone. "I'll try Logan. Does anyone have Paulette's number?"

"On it," Mara says, grabbing her phone.

We wait in heavy anticipation, but one by one, they lower their phones.

"Nothing," Austin says, slicking a hand over his forehead and looking around with wide, wild eyes. "Where could they have gone? What do we do?"

"Paulette didn't answer, either." Mara stares down at her phone.

"We have to split up," Memphis says, and the regret in his tone is heavy and palpable. "There's no choice, and we don't have time to debate. Lena and I can go one direction, you two go the other."

"No." Mara loops her arm through mine. "We can't split up. It's not safe."

"He's right," I say, and I hate it so much it stings in my chest. "We have to find them. To warn them about what happened. And without knowing which direction they headed, splitting up to cover more ground is our best option."

She looks like she wants to argue but just stares at me instead. Finally, she presses her lips together. "Then we're going together. I'm not leaving you."

"It's not safe for you two to be alone. One of us should be with you," Memphis argues.

"Why? Because we're helpless little women?" Mara shouts at him, vitriol in her voice. I know it's because she's scared. We all are. But she has a point.

"Look, we don't have time to argue. Every second we waste is a second farther away that they could be," I say, waving a hand. "It's fine. We'll head this way." I tug Mara closer to me. "You guys go that way, and if anything happens, we'll call."

Memphis looks ready to argue, but I don't give him a chance as I rattle off my phone number to him and grab Mara, leading her toward the woods on the left.

"If we stay hidden in the woods, we can walk to town," I tell her. "Try to find some help even if we don't find them.

Then we'll reconnect with the men, and I can book us another ride."

"We're going to find them, though," she whispers. "Right? We have to."

It's funny. When we arrived, I was the one who needed the assurance and comfort only Mara could give. Now, she needs it from me. I've never thought of myself as particularly brave or strong, but in the face of all this danger, the strongest emotion I have is determination.

We have to find them.

"Yeah, of course," I say, still searching everywhere for a sign of our friends or the car, hoping with everything in me to see it waiting on the side of the road, ready to rescue us.

I know it's no use. The car is gone, and I can only hope it took our friends to safety with it.

"Paulette!" We hear Austin cry from the other side of the woods, his voice loud and echoing. "Logan! Where are you guys?"

"How could the car just leave us? How could they let it?" Mara says, her voice high-pitched and breathy.

"Maybe they didn't. Maybe they didn't make it in time. Or maybe they went to get help. They wouldn't abandon us." I need her to believe it as much as I need to believe it myself. We traipse through the dark woods, leaves and sticks crunching underfoot as we struggle to make sense of the shadows.

I keep losing my sense of place, forgetting where I am and which way we came from.

Mara stops suddenly, bending forward over her knees and struggling to catch her breath. "Check and see if they made it to the car. If they were picked up. You can check in the app, can't you?"

"Oh, right." I should've thought of that. If my mind wasn't racing with fear and the need to find them, maybe I would've. Maybe I'd be thinking straight. I pull out my phone and check the app. As soon as it opens, defeat crushes me from the inside. "It shows the ride was canceled by the driver." My heart rises to my throat. If they didn't get in the car, where could they be? I don't want to think about the worst. If the neighbors caught them, they could be in the cellar with Ethan and the Hawthornes soon.

We all could.

"I'll try to call her again," Mara says, unlocking her phone screen. "Please, Paulette. Please answer."

"We need to keep moving," I warn. "Come on. We can't just stand around here waiting to get caught. We have no idea where the neighbors are or if they're coming back."

"Please, Paulette," Mara cries, holding the phone out and staring at the screen.

"Mara, come on," I beg through gritted teeth. Before I can process or make any decisions, I spot a pair of taillights on the road. Somehow, my heart both leaps with hope and freezes with trepidation in the same second.

A car is sitting on the shoulder, idling. A thick cloud of exhaust funnels out of the tailpipe.

"Is that the driver?" Mara whispers. "Could he be waiting for us?"

I swallow. "I don't know." I don't think so, but I don't want to quash her hope, even if it only lasts a second longer.

With careful, quiet steps, we cross the woods, making

our way closer to the road. When we're nearly there, I freeze, holding out a hand in front of her.

"It's the neighbors." I grab her arm and pull her backward, nearly tripping in my hurry to get away. I grab hold of a tree to stop myself from falling.

"Are you okay?" she cries, holding my arms with both of her hands.

"I'm—"

"I know you're out there..." The man's voice is closer than I expected, calling toward us from the edge of the treeline.

"Hide," I warn her, trying to pull us farther into the trees, but it's too late.

"I see you there, kids. I can hear you, too. Come on out."

I grab her hand, my feet pounding the soggy ground and wet leaves as we barrel through the woods, no longer caring about being seen or heard.

My lungs burn, and in the distance, I hear a car door shut. I have to warn Memphis and Austin. We have to find them.

What if he found Paulette and Logan? What if he got to them before we could and...

I can't allow myself to weigh the possibilities. They're just too heavy.

We make it to the road and head back toward the side of woods where the boys disappeared just as the car turns down our street, following us. He stops just before the tree as if he knew it was there. As if he chopped it down himself. I realize then, for the first time, that maybe he did.

The driver's door opens, and the man from next door steps out, staring directly into the trees where we're standing. "There you are. Didn't you hear me calling for you back there?"

What the hell? Minutes ago, he was shouting at us for being near his mailbox, and now he's acting like everything's fine. I stare at him in utter disbelief just as I hear Memphis shout.

"Lena!"

I turn my head to look for him.

"Mara!" Austin yells.

My eyes land on the two of them rushing toward us at breakneck speed, their dark figures zigzagging around trees and leaping over branches.

We could try to run, but I don't know if we'd make it. If we run, we risk splitting up again when we only just found each other. If we run, he might reach the men first. Could I risk having to live with the fact that he caught one of us or something terrible happened to them? I'm not willing to sacrifice any of my friends to save myself.

At that moment, I decide it's safer to try to convince him everything's okay. If we can just get him to leave, we'll be safe for the moment. He has no reason to suspect we know about Ethan or the Hawthornes and no reason to hurt us.

Yet.

"Sorry, we didn't hear you." I plaster a smile on my face. "We were just waiting for our ride."

Austin and Memphis reach us seconds later, both panting and out of breath.

"We should go," Memphis says firmly, moving to stand

177

in front of Mara and me. "Now." He takes a step back, trying to lead us backward up the road.

"Come on," Austin agrees.

"But go where?" the man asks. He clicks his tongue at the tree. "You know, I saw a car try to turn down this road earlier." He points behind him. "You said you were waiting for a ride? Maybe that was him. I just ran into town for a few minutes, and when I got back, this was down. No way in or out. Doesn't look like you'll be able to go anywhere except back to the house for a while. I was just pulled over on the shoulder to let my wife know what's going on. Do you need a ride somewhere? I'm happy to take you since it doesn't look like I'll be getting home with this thing anytime soon."

Staring at the car, I realize for the first time he's right. It doesn't look like there's anyone in the passenger's seat. *Where is his wife?* I check over my shoulder, half expecting her to jump out at us from behind.

Then, looking closer, I see what looks like a person sitting in the back seat. Could that be her? Why would she be in the back?

"That's okay," Memphis says. "Our ride should be here any minute."

"Yeah, thanks, though." Austin's voice trembles as he speaks.

"No problem. Are you sure? I really don't mind. Looks like we're stuck here together otherwise. I can't come through, and neither can you."

"Like he said, our driver will be here soon." I gesture down the road in the direction the imaginary car would be coming from. "And we'll be leaving with him."

"Unless he was the one who left earlier." He puts up his hands in surrender. "I think I'll just stick around and be sure he gets here safely. I couldn't live with myself if something terrible happened to you kids. You can never be too safe out here. Lots of bad apples."

I swallow, looking at Memphis. Something unspoken passes between us, and he nods his head.

"Run!" I shout, and we do. The four of us take off at lightning speed, dropping and discarding our bags as we go and darting down the street as fast as our legs will carry us.

When I glance back, the man has returned to his car. He whips it into the grass at the root of the tree, his tires spinning in the weeds, then lurches forward.

We're not going to make it. We can't outrun his car.

It's impossible.

As soon as the thought crosses my mind, it's over. He drives up ahead of us and hits his brakes. The taillights, their glowing red warning signs, tell us all that is to come... and none of it is good.

We stop in a line, arms slightly outstretched toward each other, like a mother trying to stop her child from crossing the street or slamming into the dashboard after she hits her brakes too hard.

Trying to protect each other and stay together all at once.

The man steps from the car, his face illuminated by the red glow. A thick, steady cloud of exhaust flows from the tailpipe. From where I stand, I can still see the silhouette in the back seat, though she hasn't turned around.

What is she doing? Has he hurt her again?

"I told you kids to stay away from my house," he says, eyeing us angrily.

"What did you do with Paulette and Logan?" I demand.

He glances toward the car, and my knees go weak. "I didn't do anything to them. Why don't you come over here, and I'll prove it. They're right there, safe and sound." He opens the door to the back seat, gesturing inside for them to wave at us. "Say hi to your friends, guys."

The silhouette in the back doesn't move.

"Paulette!" Mara shouts, remaining in place. "Can you hear us?"

"Paulette, are you okay?" I call, my voice hoarse and raspy from the tears burning the back of my throat. *Please, no.*

There is no movement in the car. No response.

Whoever is in the back seat doesn't budge an inch.

The man steps toward us, and we move back.

"Did you kill them?" Austin asks. "Like you killed Ethan and the other couple?"

His eyes widen, but I can't tell if he's surprised we know. He shakes his head, cocking it to the side slightly. "You snooped."

"He was our friend," Austin says, his voice cracking. "He was my best friend."

"He didn't do anything to you," I add, as it sets in further what this man has taken from me. Everything. This weekend, one of my closest friends, a future I once envisioned.

"How could you possibly know that?" he asks, tilting his head to the side.

"What do you want from us?" Mara asks, her voice shaking from where she stands next to me. I feel her hand slip into mine. "What do you want?"

He sighs. "I want to help you."

"What do you mean?" Memphis steps forward in front of us all.

"It doesn't have to be like this. Not for you, not for them." He points back toward his house. "It was never about hurting you. Any of you."

I take a step forward to stand next to Memphis, then another small step, leaning over so I can see inside the car but keeping myself at a safe distance from the man. I squint, trying to understand what I'm seeing.

From where I'm standing, I realize he was telling the truth. I can just make out Paulette's head resting against the window. As if she has passed out.

Or been knocked out.

Chills crawl up my arms.

"Oh my god." I rush forward without thinking. "Paulette! Paulette!"

The man grabs me before I reach the car, bending his knees to brace himself against the force of my weight. Memphis is there within a second, followed by Mara and Austin. The man struggles to shove me in the car, and I realize Logan is there too, his head resting in her lap.

"Let her go," Memphis shouts, trying to pull him off of me. I put my feet up against the side of the car, refusing to be shoved inside as I try to process the horror of what I'm looking at, letting it sink in for the first time.

They're dead.

Both of my friends have deep, thick red lines across

181

their throats—a single carmine slash for each of them that ended their lives. In the dark night, the cuts are practically black. Thick, sticky blood has dripped down their necks and onto their clothes. Bile rises in my throat.

I can't breathe.

They can't breathe.

He slashed their throats.

He killed them.

"Oh god," I cry as my body goes slack. I can no longer fight as the man seizes the opportunity and shoves me inside the car. "What did you do?"

No one else has noticed Paulette and Logan yet, still too busy fighting with the man, trying to pull me back out of the car. Memphis is holding on to my shoulders while either Mara or Austin tugs on my arm. Maybe both of them. I can't tell. My mind is fuzzy and the world is pure chaos. Everyone is screaming.

Suddenly, Memphis is shoved away from the car, away from me, and the man steps forward to block him from my view. I can't seem to move. It's as if I'm frozen in place.

I catch glimpses of Memphis on the ground as he wipes his bloody lip with the back of his hand and stands up again, ready to fight. I blink slowly, trying to figure out if this is really happening.

It can't be. It just can't.

"Let her go!" Memphis is shouting, but I can hardly hear him. It's as if I'm underwater, a loud ringing fills my ears, drowning everything else out.

None of this is real.

None of this is real.

None of this is real.

"You can't get us all," Memphis shouts, grabbing hold of the man's neck as he tries to pull him away from the car. "It's four against one."

"I wouldn't be so sure about that." I hear the woman's voice and know she's here, though I don't know where she came from. Memphis releases my hand, though I hadn't realized he'd been holding it, and the man steps away. But when I turn my head, it's not the woman after all.

It's Mara speaking. And Austin is standing next to her.

They're both looking at me with expressions I don't understand, expressions that feel both bitter and proud. I blink at them, my throat dry and scratchy.

"What are you—"

Before I can finish my sentence, I see the gun in her hand.

CHAPTER TWENTY-ONE

I'm dreaming. That's the only possible explanation for all of this.

Ethan is dead. Paulette and Logan are dead. Mara and Austin are helping the man take us back to the house.

The house we've been staying in.

The house we now know these people own.

Mara has a gun in her hands, which I'm just learning she kept hidden inside her bag all this time.

We are being taken against our will, and I have no idea what they're going to do to us. If we'll be dead within minutes or hours.

If I'll ever see my family again.

Something in my chest cracks at the thought of my parents wondering why I haven't come back from my trip. Waiting at the airport for my return flight. Worrying. Calling. Having to accept that I'm not coming back.

What have I done?

What is happening?

Why is this happening?

Memphis, Mara, and I are crammed into the back seat next to Logan's and Paulette's bodies while Austin rides in the front seat next to the man. I'm practically on Memphis's lap. His hands grip me tightly as he seems to try to convey so much fury and fear. I try to focus on the feel of his breath on the back of my neck. To know that I'm not completely alone. It's the only thing keeping me grounded as I realize my feet are resting on a chainsaw on the floorboard.

This was all planned.

All of it.

I glance at Mara, staring at the stranger I believed was my best friend and not wanting to believe she could do this to us. Not understanding why she would.

How could she do this to me?

How could she lie and say she was protecting me?

How could she look at my face all weekend and know what was coming?

Then, I look at Austin. In the front seat, he's staring straight ahead with his jaw set, eyes vacant and cold. I trusted him. Trusted all of them.

When I check over my shoulder, risking a glance at Memphis despite the fact that I'm not sure I can bear to look at him right now, it's clear he feels the same way.

We trusted them, and now we're going to be killed because of it. Or worse.

It's clear neither Austin nor Mara can bear to look at us or the bodies of our friends. Both are staring blankly ahead, doing everything in their power to avoid it.

I can't blame them. I can't bring myself to look at their bodies, either. Our friends. I can't make myself process the fact that they're gone. I'm actively fighting the urge to check them both for a pulse.

We're driven back to the house, and the man steps from the car, opening the back door for us to step out.

Mara points the gun in our direction, nodding for us to do what we're told. "Go."

This can't be happening. Hours ago, hell, minutes ago, I would've trusted this girl with my life. I would've fought for her. Died for her. I wasn't willing to leave her behind.

Now, she has a gun pressed into my back as we make our way into the house where we've shared so many happy moments, where I felt safe sleeping next to her just last night.

Inside, she lowers the gun, and they spread out around us. I hear the sound of footsteps before I see the woman rounding the corner from the living room. The woman I tried to protect, who I believed was dead. The woman I'd grieved because I thought I failed her. And here she is, alive and well. All of this is happening because I tried to help her. Because I cared.

"Took you long enough," she says with a sigh when Austin shuts the door, and suddenly we're cloaked in the silent stillness of the house.

"Yeah, well, your little prodigies needed some time to get it together." The man casts an angry glance our way with a flick of his wrist.

"We didn't mean to, we just... I wasn't expecting him to kill Ethan." The tears in Austin's eyes seem real. As if he might actually have a heart.

"I didn't," the man says casually. "She did. I killed the other two."

"Nathaniel!" The woman's eyes draw a line between Memphis and me. "The others? You said we'd give them more time."

"I tried, but I couldn't. They knew not only about Ethan but about Samuel and Elizabeth. They knew what we'd done." He shakes his head, massaging his temple. "I promise you, it doesn't matter. They either leave with us, or they don't leave. That's the rule. They wouldn't listen to reason. Just like my brother and that horrid wife of his. They had to be taken care of. Eradicated before they caused further harm." He takes both of her cheeks in his hands and presses a kiss to the space between her eyebrows.

"Your brother and his wife? You mean the Hawthornes?" I ask. "Samuel was your brother?"

"Unfortunately," Nathaniel says with a shrug. "But he was never worthy. He never *believed*." He holds his hand up in front of his face as he says the word, fingers pressed together as if he were mimicking a chef's kiss. "Never wanted to help me. When he thought I'd killed Vanessa, they hid in their house to confront me, but goodness always wins over evil."

"He told me he didn't know you," I say, filled with a new disgust for him. "I described you to him, told him you were staying in his house, and he must've known who you were, but he lied. You were his brother. He tried to protect you, and you killed him." I shake my head, my heart so heavy I feel like I could burst. "He was protecting you," I repeat, hoping to make it sink in. Based on the blank look I'm receiving, I know it isn't. "*How could you? That's not goodness. It's not.*" My voice is breathless and full of pain. If he's going to kill me, I want him to under-

187

stand the weight of everything he's done. "He wasn't evil. You are."

"I think you'll find you're quite wrong about that." He gives me a maniacal grin.

"What are you talking about?" Memphis asks between tight lips.

"We'll explain it all. You can give them some space," he says, and Austin and Mara step away from us at once, as if we were flames and being near us was singeing them. He waves a hand, telling us we should sit in the two chairs in the foyer.

I can't avoid looking at her anymore. I have to know. I have to hear this from her. "You were working with them the entire time?" I ask Mara, my eyes filling with tears at the betrayal. "I thought you were my best friend. I trusted you. I cared about you."

"I am, Lena," she says. "I am your best friend. I swear I care about you just as much as I always have. I'd never hurt you. I'm trying to help you."

"I don't understand." I glance down at the gun in her hand.

"You will," the woman says. When I turn to look at her, she's latched on to the man's side. "You're a good one, Lena. I knew it the second I saw you. We were in the woods that day when you first arrived, trying to understand who you were. Trying to get a feeling about all of you. And then, I saw you watching us when we were bringing food over for Ethan in the basement. I saw how you looked at me when Nathaniel and I had a disagreement about how much to feed him and how long to give him until he caught on to our message. Until he believed. Though you didn't know me, though you had no reason to want to help me, it was obvious you did. You cared about me. Just like you cared when you thought I was hurt that night."

Thought I was hurt. Suddenly, it clicks into place. "You weren't, though. The blood I saw all over you wasn't yours that night, was it?"

She sucks her teeth, squeezing her eyes shut. "That night was a mistake. I didn't mean for you to see me, see any of that. I didn't realize the curtains were open," she says. "We weren't planning to be upstairs. But it was too late. You'd already seen. So, in the heat of the moment, I dropped to the ground to make it seem like I was hurt until we came up with a game plan." She presses her lips together with a tight smile. "You must always have a plan. That's our motto."

"Whose blood was it?" I ask, knowing there can only really be one answer. My throat is dry as I croak his name. "Ethan's? That was the night you killed him? The screams I heard...it was him?"

She doesn't deny it as she casts a quick, apologetic glance at Austin and Mara.

I could've saved him. I could've stopped them. I could've done something. Anything.

"Why? Why would you kill him? I don't understand. What did he ever do to you?" I ask, my voice low. I can hardly breathe. My entire chest feels as if it's being compressed.

"We didn't want to hurt him. We never want to hurt anyone. It's never *ever* the intention. But, like my brother-in-law, he gave us no choice. After Austin recommended he book this house for your vacation, he started asking us a lot of questions. He looked us up and found out about our cause, found our web presence and discovered our beliefs. After that, he tried to get your group out of it. He wanted a refund so you could find a new place to travel. After finding out who we were, he wasn't going to allow you all to come to a house where we so strongly believe that what you are doing is wrong, but we needed you to come. We had no choice then. I had his address from the contract he'd been required to sign when he booked the house, and we tracked him down before he could tell you the truth. Before he could warn you, fill your head with lies about who we are, and convince you not to hear us out. We weren't planning to kill him, we just needed to keep him quiet long enough to make him understand. The cause is never about harm. We tried to help him, to save him. But he..." She looks at her husband, then down. "He was beyond saving. The night you saw us through the window, he was trying to escape. When I opened the basement door to collect his dishes from dinner, he'd somehow managed to untie himself and was waiting for me at the top of the stairs. He fought hard in his attempts to warn you all, but the effort was futile. He left us with no choice but to kill him. I'm so sorry you had to witness that, Lena."

"So, we were right? He's been dead since yesterday, held captive for longer," I whisper, looking at Austin. "Who was sending you those messages, then? You were just lying the whole time, weren't you?"

His cheeks grow pink. "I didn't know he was dead. I just thought they'd taken his phone while they, um, *explained* everything to him. I would text them when I needed something, and they'd send me a message from his phone. Like when I thought you were going to leave, I had them send a message from Ethan saying he was coming."

I swallow. "How could you do that?"

"It was all for the cause," he says, looking at Nathaniel with eyes full of reverence.

"The cause?" Memphis scowls. "What is this? Some fucking cult?"

The man crosses the room with four quick steps and slaps Memphis's face hard enough the sound reverberates through the space. "This is *not* a cult." Spittle forms in the corner of his mouth as he stares at him. Then he huffs a breath, runs a hand through his hair, and smooths his shirt, speaking calmly as he walks away. "We are a cause. A family. A belief system."

Memphis's chest rises and falls with heavy, angry breaths as he stares at the man, his lips pinched together.

"What is it you believe?" I ask, looking at Mara and Austin. "What is it you believe enough that it was okay to kill Ethan and Paulette and Logan? Enough that it was okay to kill our friends?"

"Sacrifices have to be made," Mara says, her chin tucked to her chest.

"What are you talking about?" I beg. "None of this makes any sense."

"What you're doing is wrong, Lena," Mara says, with so much conviction in her voice it almost convinces me.

"What do you mean? What does that mean?"

"The books you read, the things you promote. It's wrong," she says.

I jerk my head back as if I'm the one who's been slapped.

"What?" Memphis and I ask at the same time.

The man steps forward, holding up a hand to keep Mara from saying any more. He sits down on the ground in front of us, his hands steepled in front of his mouth. "Let me explain. My name is Nathaniel. You are Lena and Memphis." He nods as if telling us something we might not know. "You are *book influencers*"—he makes air quotes around the words—"meaning you promote books to the masses." He puts a hand to his chest. "But do you ever stop to think about what those books do to your heart?"

"What?" I ask, brows drawn down with an intense scowl. Nothing he's saying is making any sense.

"My heart is just fine," Memphis says. "You know, free of *literal* murder and all that."

"Ah, but it's not." Nathaniel wags a finger at him. "You are murderers. All of you. And rapists. And torturers. Thieves. My wife and I, we...we want to help you understand why this is true." He turns, holding out a hand to his wife, and she comes to join him on the ground. "This is my wife, Vanessa." He kisses her knuckles. "We used to be just like you. Lost and confused."

They smile at each other before he goes on. "We used to be readers, too. But then, it stopped feeling safe anymore. When you read terrible things, your brain can't differentiate between fiction and reality. If you read about a murder from the point of view of the murderer, your brain believes you committed a murder. If you read about a rape, you become the rapist. If you read about any sort of atrocious crime, as far as your body, as far as your nervous system, as far as your heart is concerned, you are a criminal. Don't you see?"

He pauses, his eyes bouncing back and forth between us. "Once those horrible, dark thoughts are in your head, they're in your heart, too. You'll never know they're there until it's too late. They hide out, waiting to destroy you. Waiting to suffocate you. To blacken your heart as dark as coal. We don't want to see any more young people corrupted by the written word. Our bodies were never meant to process such horrors, let alone normalize them and use them as forms of entertainment."

Suddenly, something Bertie from the bookstore said earlier replays in my mind. *You know how things are around here.* At the time, I'd thought she was referring to business being slow because it's such a small town. I'm only now realizing how wrong I've been. She meant this. This *cause.* Whatever this is. That's why her store is closing. Because of them.

I turn to Mara and Austin in a fit of rage. "And you actually believe this? Book burning and book banning, essentially? Keeping people from reading? That's what you believe in. When the world has actual problems."

"This is an actual problem, Lena. A very large one. I know it's hard to understand right now because the concept is new, but I swear to you, it's true," Vanessa says before they can answer. "Reading these kinds of books puts a darkness inside of you that's almost impossible to erase. But you can erase it, just like we have. You can join us. Help us."

"But they're book influencers, too." I wave a hand in their direction.

"They do what they have to do, what we've asked them to do, in order to help us find people like you. People who need saving. People who need to understand the harm they're causing to themselves and others. And then, when the time is right, they—like other righteous believers before them—will bring them to us so that we may begin our work toward healing them. You are our first group that Mara and Austin have brought to us. You're very, very special to them."

"I—"

"Well, I'm in," Memphis says out of nowhere.

"What?" I whip my head around to look at him.

He chews his bottom lip, nodding his head. "I mean, it makes total sense, honestly. Yeah. I'm in. I get it. Love it. Sign me up." He claps his hands together and goes to stand from the chair, but Nathaniel is up in a second, stopping him.

"I need to look into your eyes to see the truth." He bends down to Memphis's level, staring into his eyes for a long time. Their noses are just inches apart. Finally, abruptly, he turns away. "You're not a believer."

He points at Mara. "He cannot be one of us."

"Mara, no!" I cry.

She looks at the man with fear. "I—"

"He has to go, Mara," he orders. "Now."

She lifts the gun slowly, shaking her head. "I...um..."

"This is how you prove your loyalty to the cause, Mara," Vanessa says, standing up, her voice soft. "You said you could do it. You said you were ready. You promised me."

"Mara, please don't," I beg. "Please. We're your friends. You can't do this. Please. The police will be here any minute." As soon as I say it, I realize it's true.

Memphis already called them. "They'll be here, Mara. They're on their way. You haven't done anything wrong yet. You have the gun. You can stop this. You can say no and save us."

"The police aren't coming," Nathaniel says dismissively. Definitively.

"Yes. They are." I snap my head to look at him. "We called them."

"And they won't come because I've asked them not to. Otis and Ivan are good boys. They understand the cause and don't stand in my way. No one in this town does. This town believes in what we do." He folds his arms across his chest. "And those who don't...will soon."

"Speaking of," Austin says, stepping closer and lowering his voice. "Hank and Roberta almost blew our cover the first day at the market. They saw the books in Lena's bag and nearly started talking about the cause to her. I mentioned it to Memphis, and he stopped them without knowing what was really happening, but I, you know, just thought you should know."

Nathaniel smiles at him warmly, dismissing him with a wave of his hand. "I'll talk with them."

"So, what? You're taking over this town and trying to ban books and kidnap people to become part of your cul— er, cause?" Memphis demands, his upper lip curled.

"We have taken over this town, yes," Nathaniel says, "because this town was ready. The people here were ready. Soon, the world will be ready. Book bans, as you like to call them, are just the first step. The cause is great, and we are spread out all around the world, not just here. Soon, we will have done away with all books that don't align with the cause. All books with vile things in them. Only then can mankind heal."

"Mara, please," Vanessa says. "We need to move on. You've been so brave to bring them here, but they are not believers. Kill him, and we'll keep trying with her. You know some just take more coaxing than others."

"Mara," I beg, shaking my head. I move to stand in front of Memphis. "If you kill him, you'll have to kill me."

Fat tears fill her eyes as she stares at me. "Don't make me do this, Lena. Please. I have to do what he says."

Memphis holds on to my waist, his lips pressing into my hair. For a second, I think he's on board with the plan.

Then, I feel him kiss the top of my head. "Run."

"Wha—"

Before I can ask, he shoves me forward and darts away, launching toward Mara, who is too shocked to do anything but scream. He knocks her to the ground, and the gun slides across the floor. I dive for it, but Austin is quicker. He kicks it out of the way, and it goes under a sofa in the small sitting room off the foyer.

"Get it!" Nathaniel yells as Austin, Vanessa, and I charge for the gun.

I launch myself onto the ground, reaching and searching for the cold metal, but I don't feel it. In one swift move, Austin overturns the sofa, and I scramble for it, but he's faster. He bends and grabs it, spinning on his heel to face us.

"Austin, please," I beg, staring into the eyes of someone I considered a friend just hours ago.

How did we get here?

For a moment, I'm not sure he knows what he's going to do.

"For Ethan," I squeak. "For Logan and Paulette. For our friends."

"We had to do it, Austin," Vanessa says, taking a step toward him. "We had to kill them. You know that. For the cause."

I bite my lip, fighting back tears. "They loved you, Austin. Ethan loved you. He considered you his friend. His best friend. Like Mara is mine."

"He trusted you," Memphis adds from across the room. "Thought of you as a brother. He wouldn't want you to do this. You can let us go to honor him."

"Just let us go," I beg. "Please, Austin. Please let us go."

"If you let them go, they'll tell. They'll ruin everything," Nathaniel points out. "Everything we've worked so hard for. Everything you've trained for."

"They killed Ethan," I whisper. "They looked him in the eyes and killed him in cold blood. Paulette and Logan, too. We're not the monsters here, Austin. No matter what they tell you. The things that they're talking about, the things they say get inside your head, and you don't know they're there until they hurt you... It's not books, it's people like this." I wave a hand in their direction. "Like them. People who try to convince you that something you love is bad. That people should have to suffer for the greater good. That words on a piece of paper, meant to entertain or enlighten or teach, could ever be as evil as the man holding a gun."

Austin wavers, lowering the gun slightly.

"You don't want to do this," I add. "*We* are your

friends, Austin. Not them. Reading dark books may show us terrible things, but they show us good things, too. Great things. Friends, family, love... Good wins in the end. People make the right choices. Justice prevails. You have to see the bad to appreciate the good, but that doesn't make it wrong."

"Don't listen to her, Austin," Nathaniel says, moving closer to him. "We're your family. We love you. The cause is all about love."

Austin locks eyes with him, slowly raising the gun, almost as if in a trance.

"Austin, listen, I, um..." Memphis's voice is too loud. I turn to face him as he stumbles around his words, looking down, then back up to meet my eyes. He takes several slow steps backward. "Hey, look. Listen. Listen. I get what you guys are doing. Truly, I do. I think there's a better way, but I've told you, I don't even really like thrillers. There's this one book that I...that I recommend to everyone." He stops, his eyes locked on mine, and he cocks his head to the side, then turns to look out the window.

This one book that I recommend to everyone.

I get it. I know what he's doing.

I understand what he's asking of me.

The brutal ending to *Of Mice and Men* plays out in my head. The distraction. If I'm right, he's going to cause a distraction.

Like clockwork, he shouts, "Holy shit, you guys, the cops are here. The FBI. Dark cars. SWAT teams. Shit, shit, shit!"

"What?" Nathaniel and Vanessa lurch forward, rushing to push Memphis out of the way. Without a second to spare, I launch forward and shove into Austin, taking the gun without a hint of a struggle. It's almost like he's glad to let it go.

He drops to the ground, both hands out in front of him, waiting for the police. Waiting for the end.

Before Nathaniel and Vanessa realize what's happened, the tables have turned. I hold the gun and point it directly at Nathaniel. He's the head of the snake, and as long as he's here, this will never end.

Aim for the head.

"Austin, stop her!" Nathaniel cries, but Austin doesn't move from his place on the ground.

"You know what's funny?" I ask, staring at them with disdain as I grind my teeth together. "We learned that old trick from a book."

I pull the trigger.

CHAPTER TWENTY-TWO

ONE YEAR LATER

I walk into Spines and Wines just after nine in the morning, a paper cup of coffee already in my hand. My heels click across the tile floor as I make my way through the building, the scent of warm coffee and books hitting my nose.

Even after everything, it's still my favorite scent in the world.

"Morning, Mary," I say, waving a hand at her. Today, her hair has been dyed a bright shade of aquamarine. "Love that new color on you."

She looks up at me with wide eyes and puts down the book she was reading, running a hand over her hair. "Well, hey, stranger. I didn't know you were coming by today. How've you been?"

"Oh, fine. Staying busy, all that. How about you? You just got back from the Bahamas, didn't you?"

She grins. "You remembered! Yes, I did. Now that we've got Allen trained"—she points to the man with gray hair tucked under his tweed cap who's carefully restocking shelves across the store—"I can actually take vacation time without worrying about that old grump in his office back there. I'd forgotten what that feels like."

"So you had a nice time?"

"The best." She beams.

"I'm glad. You deserved it. And, speaking of *that old grump*, I was hoping to catch him if he's in the office today." I run a hand through Lenny's soft fur as the fat cat raises her head to look at me, then lies back down and continues purring. "He's not expecting me, but I brought treats." I lift the cup in the air.

She tilts her head toward his office and lowers her voice. "You came at the right time. He just got off a call. Go on in. Want me to tell him you're here?"

"Nah, I'll just pop in. You're the best." I cross the book-store at a leisurely pace, perusing the shelves for anything new. I stop at each of the memorial shelves, running my fingers over the nameplates Memphis and I had made in memory of our dear friends who gave their lives in the name of books.

Paulette. On her shelf, there are plenty of romance books and a few spicy thrillers.

Logan. I run my fingers across the collection of The Hardy Boys novels and other mysteries.

Ethan. I stop at his shelf, running a finger over the spine of the last book he reviewed. One he'd begged me to buddy read with him, though I hadn't had the time. Memphis has also filled his shelf with all of his favorites from Lyra James.

It's not much. Not nearly enough. But it's something we could do. Some small thing to let the world and their families know they aren't forgotten.

It never gets easier, knowing they're gone.

Knowing how senseless it all was. How easily it could've been anyone else. Often, I find myself wondering if we should've left sooner. If I could've done more to save us.

If they'd still be here if I made a single different decision.

I'll never know, and I think for the rest of my life, that will kill me.

"Hey, Allen."

"Hello there, Lena. Looking mighty pretty today."

I wave him off. "Oh, you old flirt." When I reach Memphis's door, I knock twice, then push it open. "Knock, knock."

"I'm not buying," he says, standing up with a sly grin when he sees it's me.

"Lucky for you, I'm not selling." I walk around his desk and give him a tight hug, breathing in the scent I've become so accustomed to.

"It's good to see you, Lena."

"It's really good to see you, too. I'm sorry I haven't been around much this...*month?* Has it been a month? Wow, I'm awful." I press a fist into my hip.

He shrugs, sitting down in the oversized executive chair I bought him for his birthday after insisting he throw away the one that was killing his back. I found out later he'd just taken it back to his apartment, but it was a nice first step. "Well, I'll let you off the hook because I'm awful, too. It *has* been a month, and I know this because I was out of town the week before last, and last week was Mary's vacation, so I was swamped. We're both to blame."

"Equal blame," I say, bobbing my head. "I like it." He

flashes me one of those smiles I'm seeing more and more often. "How've you been?"

"It's picking up. The new Stephen King book just released, so there's always a nice little boom." He raps his knuckles on his desk. "And Mary convinced me to order some new seasonal flavors for the store's coffee, which have actually been a big hit."

"I didn't ask how the store has been," I point out, realizing I'm still standing and finally sitting down in the chair across from him. "I asked how *you* have been. You do know you're two separate things, don't you? There is a place where you end and the store begins."

He chuckles. "I've been told." With a sudden grimace, he eyes my cup. "Did you actually come in here with coffee when you know we have the best. What is wrong with you?"

"Ah, ah, ah. You won't be able to say you have the best for long." I slide the cup across to him. "Try this."

He studies the cup but doesn't move to take it. "Why?"

"It's not poisoned," I say with a laugh. "Don't worry, my latest Agatha Christie didn't put too much of a black smudge on my heart just yet."

"Too soon," he says, shaking his head at the dark joke. "Way, way too soon." Lifting the cup to his lips, he takes a hesitant sip of the coffee. He pulls his head back, eyeing the cup. "This is good. This is actually really, really good. Where'd you get it?"

"The new little bookstore that's getting ready to open up like six blocks down. Cup and Page. Have you heard of it?"

He scowls. "Oh. Yeah, I have."

I shrug one shoulder. "Well, what do you say? Are you up for a little friendly competition?"

It takes him a second to process what I've said. "Wait... No. You didn't."

"I did." I grin with my tongue pressed to my top teeth.

"You own the bookstore? Seriously? You bought a building and became my rival? Why didn't you tell me?"

"*Leased*, technically," I correct, a finger in the air. Then, I slap his desk and grab the cup, taking a drink myself. "The world needs more bookstores, my friend."

His eyes darken with meaning at the word *friend*. We both know we've been teetering on the edge of something more, but with the chaos of last year, it hasn't felt right.

"Why didn't you tell me you were doing this?"

"Well, *technically*, I *did* tell you I was thinking about opening a bookstore since I'm wildly attracted to the owner of this one and can't work here."

He blanches. "I thought you were joking."

"About which part?"

His lips pinch together. "Lena."

"Well, I wanted to be certain everything was going to work out, and then it just became a fun surprise. Besides, we're not really rivals. We're all working together, aren't we? Building an army of readers with black hearts." I pat my chest. "And I didn't know if you had any rules about competing with people you were insanely attracted to." I wrinkle my nose.

"Hmm. Can't say that I do," he teases, folding his arms across his chest. "In fact, healthy competition—I guess it could be sort of fun."

"Well, good, because I'm also helping Bertie keep her

bookstore open, and I didn't want the attraction between the two of you to get too awkward."

He shakes his head, swiping the cup of coffee back from me and taking another drink.

I giggle. "Seriously, though, I think if we can make a few changes and restructure a bit, it will help keep her afloat."

He runs a hand across his face. "Well, I'm glad you're helping her. That place can't afford to lose its only bookstore."

"No. There's still work to be done, but with Nathaniel dead and Vanessa in prison, the area—hell, the world—is better off. *The cause* is gone. We did it, my friend. Saved the world."

He eyes me, leaning back in his seat. "For now, maybe. But we both know there will always be a new *cause*. Austin and Mara are in therapy, but what happens if they decide to pick up where their bosses left off? Or any of the other people out there who Nathaniel warned us about? There have been over three thousand books banned this year so far. He said it was just the beginning, and I don't think he was lying. Someone else will always be out there trying to stop people from reading. They aren't giving up."

"Fine, sure." I nod. "*But* we're not giving up, either. We'll be here to stop them. One *cup* and one *page* at a time."

Chuckling, he lifts the cup and takes a sip thoughtfully, then reaches across the desk and laces his fingers with mine. "That we will. After all, spoiler alert: in the end, good wins."

I squeeze his hand, knowing how true his words are, how true they'll always be. "In the end, good wins."

WOULD YOU RECOMMEND YOU'LL NEVER KNOW I'M HERE?

If you enjoyed this story, please consider leaving me a quick review. It doesn't have to be long—just a few words will do. Who knows? Your review might be the thing that encourages a future reader to take a chance on my work! To leave a review, please visit: kierstenmodglinauthor.com/youllneverknowimhere

Let everyone know how much you loved *You'll Never Know I'm Here* on Goodreads: https://bit.ly/youllneverknowimhere

STAY UP TO DATE ON EVERYTHING KMOD!

Thank you so much for reading this story. I'd love to invite you to sign up for my mailing list and text alerts so we can be sure you don't miss my next release.

Sign up for my mailing list here:
kierstenmodglinauthor.com/nlsignup

Sign up for my text alerts here:
kierstenmodglinauthor.com/textalerts

ACKNOWLEDGMENTS

I am forever in awe of and very grateful for the beautiful book community. I consider myself so fortunate to be surrounded by such enthusiastic readers, who not only love to read, but love to talk about what they're reading.

When I was a little girl, books were an escape for me. They were a way for me to feel like I fit in somewhere when I so often felt like I didn't fit in where I was. Books made me feel seen and they made me feel less alone. My favorite moments were (and still are) when I'd come across a passage with a completely obscure experience or thought I could relate to and I'd realize none of us are as alone as we think we are.

Aside from my grandmothers, a cousin, and one or two of my friends, I never truly had anyone to talk with about the books I was reading and the things I was experiencing. So, while I know the internet can be a scary and, frankly, terrible place at times, it's also really beautiful. It has given me a place, a community, and a family among my fellow book people.

People who fall in love with fictional characters, who cry over losses that only exist on the page, and who spend every night reading just "one more chapter" over and over again.

The book community that I have found since I've

become a writer is full of some of the most kind, gracious, and absolutely magical people I've ever had the pleasure of meeting, and when I decided to write this book, I wanted it to be for them.

This novel was my love letter to books and to reading. I filled it with some of my own "bookish confessions" (though NOT all of them are mine!), thoughts I have about bookstores and books in general, my own experiences with reading, and the love that I feel for the online book community and the stories that bring us together.

If you're here and reading this, if you're a part of that online community, if you spend your time spreading book love rather than hate, and if you encourage others to read any book you're enjoying, this book is for you. And for me. And for the stories we love, the tales we get lost in, and the pages where we somehow seem to find ourselves.

I also need to say thank you to the following people who, just like books, make me feel much less alone in the world:

To the world's best husband and sweetest little girl— thank you for being by my side through everything. I'm so grateful to get to do life with you both. You make every day an adventure and I love you so much.

To my incredible editor, Sarah West—thank you for all you do for my stories! I'm so thankful for your advice, guidance, and insight. Thank you for always seeing the story I'm trying to tell and helping me to get there.

To the awesome proofreading team at My Brother's Editor—thank you for being the final set of eyes on my stories and helping to polish them until they shine! I'm very grateful to have you on the team!

To my loyal readers (AKA the #KMod Squad)—thank you so much for…well, everything! You have changed my life in the most unimaginable ways. I'm so incredibly grateful for the ways you show up for me time and time again. Thank you for believing in me, cheering me on, returning for story after story, and giving little Kiersten everything she ever wished for. All my life, I've dreamed of having someone to tell these stories in my head to. I just never imagined I'd be lucky enough to get all of you. I love you guys so much!

To my book club/gang/besties—Sara, both Erins, June, Heather, and Dee—LADIES!!! Thank you for showing up for me when it isn't easy or convenient, for being the ones I go to when I need to talk or cry or vent. Thank you for making me feel seen and loved and supported through every chapter of this wild journey. I'm so grateful for the little family we've built, for the laughs and tears and everything in between. I love you all.

To my bestie, Emerald O'Brien—thank you for being the first person I get to tell about every idea I have, the first one to read my stories, and the one who champions each and every page. My biggest cheerleader, strongest defender, and the one who always knows what to say or how to fix that massive plot hole. I couldn't do any of this without you. Love you, friend. Same moon.

To Becca and Lexy—thank you for keeping me above water on days when it feels like I'm drowning. I'm so grateful for your support, for the laughs, and for your friendship.

To the online book community—thank you for all you have done for me, my stories, and my career. I love you and am so grateful for the way you have introduced my books to the world in ways I never dreamed possible.

Last but certainly not least, to you, dear reader—thank you for purchasing this book and supporting my art. I can't tell you how much it means to me. As a young girl with her head stuck in a book, all I wished for, all I dreamed of and hoped for and thought of, was how much I hoped someday someone would purchase a book with my name on it. That someone would want to read a story I'd written. So thank you for making that and so many other dreams come true for me. Whether this is your first Kiersten Modglin book or your 42nd, my greatest wish is that it was everything you hoped for and nothing like you expected.

ABOUT THE AUTHOR

KIERSTEN MODGLIN is a Top 10 bestselling author of psychological thrillers. Her books have sold over a million copies and been translated into multiple languages. Kiersten is a member of International Thriller Writers, Novelists, Inc., and the Alliance of Independent Authors. She is a KDP Select All-Star and a recipient of *ThrillerFix's* Best Psychological Thriller Award, *Suspense Magazine's* Best Book of 2021 Award, a 2022 Silver Falchion for Best Suspense, and a 2022 Silver Falchion for Best Overall Book of 2021. Kiersten grew up in rural western Kentucky and later relocated to Nashville, Tennessee, where she now lives with her family. Kiersten's readers across the world lovingly refer to her as "KMod." A binge-watching expert, psychology fanatic, and *indoor* enthusiast, Kiersten enjoys rainy days spent with her favorite people and evenings with her nose in a book.

Sign up for Kiersten's newsletter here:
kierstenmodglinauthor.com/nlsignup

Sign up for text alerts from Kiersten here:
kierstenmodglinauthor.com/textalerts

kierstenmodglinauthor.com
www.facebook.com/kierstenmodglinauthor
www.facebook.com/groups/kmodsquad
www.twitter.com/kmodglinauthor
www.instagram.com/kierstenmodglinauthor
www.tiktok.com/@kierstenmodglinauthor
www.goodreads.com/kierstenmodglinauthor
www.bookbub.com/authors/kiersten-modglin

<u>STANDALONE NOVELS</u>

Becoming Mrs. Abbott

The List

The Missing Piece

Playing Jenna

The Beginning After

The Better Choice

The Good Neighbors

The Lucky Ones

I Said Yes

The Mother-in-Law

The Dream Job

The Nanny's Secret

The Liar's Wife

My Husband's Secret

The Perfect Getaway

The Roommate

The Missing

Just Married

Our Little Secret

Widow Falls

Missing Daughter

The Reunion

Tell Me the Truth

The Dinner Guests

If You're Reading This...

A Quiet Retreat

The Family Secret

Don't Go Down There

Wait for Dark

You Can Trust Me

Hemlock

Do Not Open

You'll Never Know I'm Here

ARRANGEMENT TRILOGY

The Arrangement (Book 1)

The Amendment (Book 2)

The Atonement (Book 3)

THE MESSES SERIES

The Cleaner (Book 1)

The Healer (Book 2)

The Liar (Book 3)

The Prisoner (Book 4)

NOVELLAS

The Long Route: A Lover's Landing Novella

The Stranger in the Woods: A Crimson Falls Novella

Made in the USA
Columbia, SC
08 December 2023

28044682R00136